TAKING ROOT

A CANDLEWOOD FALLS NOVEL

STACEY WILK

STACEY WILK

This book is dedicated to the loving memory of my beautiful friend and award winning author, Marykate Schweiger.
"I love you, madly."

~

HAVE WE GOT A STORY FOR YOU!

Dear Readers:

Welcome to Candlewood Falls!

Each Candlewood Falls story stands alone. However, the end of one story doesn't mean the end of your favorite characters. They can show up in any Candlewood Falls book at any time.

Candlewood Falls is a unique world of connected stories by different authors whose characters, business, and events appear in each others' stories.

Think of Candlewood Falls as a literary soap opera.

Be sure to check out the Ready For Another Trip to Candlewood Falls page at the end to discover which other books include your favorite characters.

Happy reading!

Stacey Wilk, K.M Fawcett, & Jen Talty

∽

CHAPTER ONE

The pounding against the front door, in the middle of the night, made her reach for the shotgun. Brooklyn Wilde didn't have any idea how to work the gun, or any idea who was at the door—because it must be a fist making that thumping noise—but she did have an idea that whoever it was could not be there to sell cookies. She only wished she had listened to Cordy when her grandmother had offered a lesson in firearm usage.

The urgent knocking continued. The rain pelted the roof and swept angry strokes against the living room window. Not a great night to be out, let alone paying an uninvited visit. Brooklyn's hands shook as she debated her next move. Her shoulders ached with the weight of the gun and her indecision. If she strained to hear, one of the alpacas screeched from the nearby barn. Probably Lucy trying to warn her about the unwanted guest.

"Thanks, Lucy." For a moment she wished the alpacas were Rottweilers because right now she lived alone in the big farmhouse. She could call the police, but her phone was upstairs in the bedroom.

She crept through the living room in her bare feet, the floor cold against her skin, her gaze trained on the door. The clock on the mantel chimed midnight. She jumped and almost put a hole in the ceiling.

The pounding stopped, but the rain continued its primal beat. She let out a huge breath and relaxed her grip on the heavy gun. Maybe the person gave up and went back out to the road. But what if they were hurt? Her years as a nurse wanted to kick in—she was trained to help—but she fought the urge. After the attack last year, she stayed away from strangers. As long as the knocking didn't continue, she'd assume whoever had been outside had had the wrong house. Not exactly easy to do considering the farm was set back from the road quite a distance and butted up against her family's apple orchard on one side, but she'd go with the theory no knocking meant nobody.

Maybe she should call her brother and have him walk the property, just in case. If Brad was good at anything it was looking menacing. She turned for the stairs.

The hammering resumed and froze her to the spot. She couldn't move, but her brain yelled to run. She could scream, but no one would hear her. *Move*, she willed her legs. *Go get the damn phone.*

"Is anyone home…please…I could use a little help." A deep male voice accompanied the assault on the door. The voice was strained and halting as if each syllable cost him effort. This person might be hurt after all.

She aimed the gun at the door again. "I have a shotgun, and I'm not afraid to use it." Pulling the trigger scared her almost as much as the stranger on the other side of the door. She wasn't in the habit of hurting people, but she would put a bullet in this guy if it meant she might get attacked again. "Just turn around and head back to the road, and you won't get hurt." Her throat closed against her words, strangling them. She hoped she sounded more confident than she felt.

"I'm already hurt. I don't have a phone. I can't walk back to the road. The rain is coming down hard."

"Not my problem, pal. I'll call nine-one-one for you, but that's it. Now start walking before I blow a hole through my grandmother's door." Which she would, if forced to. She was done being a victim.

"Brooklyn, is that you?"

Her heart nearly stopped. He knew her name, this stranger standing on the porch on a terrible night. Did he really know her? Or had he stalked her? The man who had attacked her last year had been caught, but was he free and here in Candlewood Falls?

She inched closer to the door. If this guy were a friend of her brother's he would've said that. If this man were a friend of her father's, he could probably stitch himself up with one eye closed and have a CB signal out for medical attention from a group of people with very special interests. He must know her somehow, or he was lying.

"Hello? Brooklyn? Please open the door. It's Caleb Ransom."

Caleb Ransom? Why would he be in town, in the middle of the night? As far as she knew, he hadn't stepped foot in Candlewood Falls since his arrest twelve years ago. They hadn't spoken since then either. Her family didn't want her keeping in touch with the man who had killed her uncle.

She put the gun down and shifted the curtain just enough to peek out the window. The night was black as ink. Except for the cone of golden light coming from above the barn and casting the porch in shadows, she couldn't see much.

She moved to get a better look. Sure enough, a man stood on the porch. He was tall and lean. He rested his forehead on his arm, blocking a good look at his face. How was she supposed to know if this was Caleb? And what if it wasn't? She would be opening her door to another attacker. She wiped her palms on her thighs.

"Prove to me that you're really Caleb." She inched closer to the door and grabbed the gun but pointed it at the ceiling this time. She didn't want to accidentally shoot him.

"Come on. If I'm not Caleb, why would I pretend to be? Who the hell wants to be me in this backwards town? Please, Brooklyn. I'm bleeding. I fell off my motorcycle. I don't think I can stand up anymore." His words rattled like ice in a glass as he spoke.

He also had a point. Most people from his past still believed he had beat SJ Wilde to death even though Caleb had been released from prison. He hadn't been totally exonerated, though. The authorities had turned him loose on a technicality. But she had believed him.

"Why did you come here?" She moved closer to the door. He could've gone to Doc's for medical attention.

"I was driving by. I got caught off guard by some asshole in a hurry, and I spun out. When I realized I was near Cordy's farm, I came down the drive." Cordy had always liked Caleb as much as Brooklyn had. She had never believed he murdered Brooklyn's uncle SJ.

"Let me call an ambulance for you."

"No, don't. Please. An ambulance will bring the police. The police don't like me. I have nowhere else to go, and I can't make it back to town to drag that old doctor out of his bed. I need a few bandages and maybe some aspirin. A chance to warm up and dry off. Then I'll go if you want me to." The rain thumping on the roof was no match for the clamorous pain in his voice.

Opening the door could be a huge mistake, but it wouldn't be her first. She had made plenty of mistakes in her life, and that was why she was even in her grandmother's house to begin with. Cordy had taken her in with open arms because her life had fallen apart expertly.

The brass bolt chilled her already cold fingers. With a final hesitation, it twisted under her influence, and she opened the door, waiting for something or someone to pounce, expecting to be fooled.

Instead, Caleb stared back at her with one eye swollen shut. Blood ran under his nose and around his chin. Some of it had made its way onto his shirt. His left cheek was an ugly purple, and his lip was split.

"Come inside." She reached for him, but he flinched. She stepped back, giving him some space the way she would if one of the alpacas had a thorn in their paw.

"I think the person in the car may have been following me." He limped through the doorway and fell to his knees as if the threatening wind pushed him down. A puddle of water mixed with blood pooled on the hardwood floor.

"I better call for help." She slammed the door shut and locked it.

"No, don't. I'll be okay." He struggled to get to his feet, but his foot slipped.

"At least let me help you." She wrapped an arm around his waist and detected a hint of whiskey. His wet clothes soaked through her thin nightgown. She barely came to his shoulder, making him lean over in order for her to support his weight and nearly sending them both to the ground. She tried to help him a second time, draping his arm over her shoulder to keep him upright.

"I can walk." He eased out of her embrace.

"Yeah, that's apparent." And as stubborn as ever.

A little strangled laugh fell off his lips. He winced. "Still the same Brooklyn, always speaking her mind." He dropped onto the sofa with huff.

"I'll be right back." She ran to the mudroom for clean

towels and some kind of medical supplies. They had plenty of things to clean up cuts. Living and working on an alpaca farm often meant someone needed anything from a bandage to tweezers for removing a splinter.

She rummaged through the first aid kit. Caleb had said she was still the same. She was anything but the same girl who had left Candlewood Falls twelve years ago. She wasn't even the same person she was a year ago. If she had been, she wouldn't be standing in her grandmother's mudroom looking for hydrogen peroxide to help a broken Caleb Ransom. She found what she needed, gathered everything in her arms, and returned to the living room.

Caleb leaned his head back on the couch. His eyes were closed. He didn't move. She pressed her fingers against his chilled neck.

"I'm not dead." He lifted his head and grabbed her hand. He stared right through her with his warm dark-brown eyes. A familiar shiver ran over her skin as she held his gaze, but she pulled her hand away.

"I'm going to clean you up. Are you hurt anywhere else?" She knelt down beside him and opened the hydrogen peroxide. His arms were cut in several places, but the lacerations were small and already clotting. He was responsive with his sense of humor intact. His face seemed the worst of it so far.

He lifted his shirt and revealed scrapes the size of tall reeds alongside his rib cage. A bruise already discolored his skin around the injury. He could have a bruised rib. She didn't think it was broken. His breathing wasn't labored enough for that.

She held up the bottle and the cotton. "I'm going to need to get some bandages too." She went back and grabbed the box of latex bandages.

She should be a little worried, kneeling down in front of Caleb. Even in his state, he could overpower her. She shook the thought away. If he were going to hurt her, would he show up here beaten this badly just as a ploy? Wouldn't it have been easier to corner her in an alley or behind a bar? Like the way her uncle SJ had died. She needed to stop. Caleb wasn't a killer. She knew him back then. She knew him well. He wasn't the kind of man who lurked in the shadows and pounced, taking away dignity and the illusion of safety.

He stopped her hands before she could reach his face with her medicinal supplies. His hands were strong and calloused. He had done a lot of physical labor by the looks of his scratched and scarred fingers. He took the dry cotton and pressed it against the end of his nose to stop the bleeding.

"Thanks. The bleeding has stopped mostly. If I could clean up some, I'll be fine." He shifted on the couch and winced again, grabbing his side.

"You don't look fine. Are you sure you don't want to go to the hospital? It's not that far. I can drive you." She moved from her spot so close to him. She hadn't been that close to a man in months. A little space would keep her head clear in order to figure out what to do with him.

"No hospitals. Would it be too much to ask for a hot shower? I really want to get out of these wet clothes." He rolled his head on his neck and set off a cacophony of snaps and cracks.

"Did you see the car that cut you off?" She rubbed away some of the blood that had clung to her fingers. Bile rose in her throat; she was unable to completely stomach the sight of blood any longer.

"It was a dark sedan. Could be one in a million." He explored the swelling around his eye and flinched.

"Ice. You need ice. What the hell was I thinking?" She ran into the kitchen and gathered ice into a dish towel. "Here." She was out of practice and not in any hurry to return to the world of nursing. She no longer wished to witness people rolling into the emergency room on stretchers, bleeding and battered from any number of things.

"Thank you. But how about that shower? I want to get this stink off me." He placed the ice on his swollen eye.

Caleb in her shower. How was she contemplating this? But she was. She shuddered from the thought but also from the cold. Her cotton pajamas were wet now and sticking to her. A quick glance told her she was on display more than she cared to be. She grabbed one of Cordy's blankets she had made from alpaca fleece and wrapped it around her, sinking into its warmth and giving her a barrier from Caleb.

"Don't you want to file a police report or something?" She didn't know if she wanted him in her shower. It didn't seem right to send him back out into the night in his condition, but she wasn't sure if allowing him to stay any longer was a good idea either. After all these years, he had become a stranger, and she didn't want to be around anyone she didn't know anymore. Funny how one little attack could change an entire world view.

If Cordy were here, she would have the tub filling and chicken soup on the stove, because Cordy believed the best in everyone. But she wasn't here. Brooklyn had to decide on her own if she was safe with Caleb in the house. Him naked in her shower would give her an advantage. She did have the shotgun as well.

He arched a brow. "A police report? What good would that do?"

"I guess nothing." She pulled the blanket closer and eyed the shotgun. She could let Caleb stay in the barn for the night. The alpacas wouldn't mind the company.

He followed her gaze and pushed off the couch, but it took two tries to stand straight. Sweat popped out on his forehead from the effort. "I can tell I'm making you uncomfortable. I thought because Cordy believed I was innocent maybe you would too. My mistake. I'll get out of your hair. Thanks for the ice and the cotton." He wiped his brow and swayed on his feet. "It's warm in here."

"Caleb, you need the hospital. You might have a head injury. You could be bleeding internally. Let me take you to Doc's at least."

"No doctor."

He shuffled a few steps before his eyes rolled into the back of his head, and he collapsed to the ground with a thud.

"Caleb?" She dropped down beside him. He didn't move. "Well, shit."

CHAPTER TWO

The pounding in Caleb's head woke him with a jolt. He groaned and blinked against the sunlight streaming through the windows. Sunlight. It was dark when he had arrived at Cordy's place. He sat up, but the room spun and knocked him back onto the soft mattress. Every inch of his body ached. He had taken some beating last night when he fell off his motorcycle. He had only wanted to get on to the next town. He should never have stopped for that drink at Murphy's, the tavern in town. When he had left, the sedan had pulled out right behind him. He had known better than to stick around Candlewood Falls, but he had decided to get sentimental.

He took stock of his surroundings. He must still be at Cordy's because the last thing he remembered was struggling to get off the couch so he could leave and telling Brooklyn not to call Doc.

She must've moved him to a small bedroom. The paneled walls were painted a light green. The hardwood floor was old and worn, but rugs of different sizes and colors covered the floor in a random pattern. The windows were wide and allowed way too much light in the room. The gauzy curtains did nothing to shield his eyes.

He had planned to limp back to his twisted-up motorcycle and push it out of town. He could've found a motel for the night. Brooklyn hadn't been able to hide her unease around him. He didn't blame her. The last time they had spoken was through the bars of a jail cell. He might not have knocked on this door if he had known she was here. He had fully expected Cordy to let him in. Cordy never treated him any differently. Even when he had been accused of killing SJ Wilde, her son-in-law's brother.

He lifted the floral comforter draped over his legs and groaned. He also didn't remember taking his clothes off. Only his underwear remained. How did that waif of a woman get him into bed and out of his clothes? And where were his clothes?

His jeans were folded neatly on the white rocking chair. His black duffel waited patiently near the chair. If his duffel was here, then she went out to the road where he had left his bike. His scratched-up boots were placed on the floor beside the chair as if that were their rightful place. He wanted to laugh at the idea, but the effort hurt his sore ribs. Probably a bruise. Hopefully, nothing more.

He eased off the bed and stuck his legs in his pants. The pain in his head throbbed. He didn't see the t-shirt he wore last night, but he had a few others with him. He'd quickly dress and leave before Brooklyn started looking for him. Coming here had been a dumb idea, but it was nice to see her again.

He had hoped that maybe Brooklyn wouldn't look at him as if he were a killer. When she had been the one on the other side of the door, he had hoped she would see the world the way her grandmother did and not judge him. All he needed was a place where he wouldn't be judged for a crime he hadn't committed.

"Are you out of your mind?" a male voice echoed from the other room.

Caleb stopped short with one foot hovering above his boot.

"What I do is none of your business," Brooklyn said. A husband or boyfriend maybe? He hadn't seen a ring on her finger last night, but he wasn't exactly on the top of his game then.

"It is if it's on Cordy's farm."

"The farm doesn't belong to you. Go back to the orchard and throw your weight around there."

She was talking to her twin brother. Caleb ran a hand through his hair—even that hurt. He wasn't ready to see Brad Wilde. He just wanted to sneak out of the house, get his bike, and put as many miles as possible between him and Candlewood Falls. Whoever had followed him in the sedan, had tailed him. Their high beams had reflected in his side mirrors, making it hard to see. The rain that had come up unexpectedly had also made driving difficult. He had known he was in trouble when the sedan passed him in the no passing zone. Whoever was in that car had to know who he was and was sending him a message. *Get out. You're still not wanted here.* That was fine. He had no intention of staying.

Candlewood Falls had been his home once. He liked growing up on a farm even though he was nothing more than a caretaker's son. He had wished, a long time ago, he could put roots down here, but bad timing had ruined that plan. Now, he snuck into town once a year to visit his mother's grave. He came late at night so no one would notice him. And then he left as fast as he arrived.

"I want him out of here, now." Brad didn't seem to care

that his voice carried right through the thin walls. Or he knew exactly what he was doing, hoping to be heard.

Caleb grabbed his duffel and took a deep breath. He could climb out the window and make a run for it, but he was tired of running and hiding. He hadn't done anything wrong. He had never hurt SJ. He had never hurt anyone who hadn't laid a hand on him first. And Brooklyn was a grown woman. If she saw fit to disrobe him and let him sleep in her bed, well her brother would just have to deal with it.

The bedroom door creaked on its hinges. The arguing in the other room stopped on a dime. He couldn't turn around now. Instead, he tried to cover up his limp and squared his shoulders at the sight of Brad Wilde scowling in his direction.

"Oh, good. You're up. I made breakfast. I hope you're hungry." Brooklyn's smile spread wide. She had on a long dark-orange sweater that made her cheeks glow and jeans that hugged her legs. Her feet were bare. Her feet and legs had been bare last night when she came to the door and let him in. Even in his messed-up state, he hadn't missed how little her pajamas hid.

The kitchen was bright with yellow walls and shelves for cabinets. The plates and cups lining the shelves were in many colors. Everything in here spoke of Cordy with her flowered curtains on the window and the plants lining the sill. The only thing that didn't seem to fit were him and Brad's contorted face.

"I can't stay, but thank you." He held his gaze on Brooklyn's and still the heat climbed up his neck. He didn't belong here. He had been a fool to think anything would be different for him. He wasn't wanted here. But the smell of eggs cooking in melting butter tempted him to stay a little longer.

"Well, that's good because my sister isn't in the business of taking in strays." Brad narrowed his eyes. He was a big guy with broad shoulders and thick arms from slogging labor on the apple orchard right alongside the men who worked for him. The tattoos and the hair to his shoulders only added to the intimidating look.

"Shut up." Brooklyn threw a wooden spoon at Brad who ducked in time. The spoon fell to the floor with a rattle.

"Do what you want with this one because you're going to anyway." Brad hitched a thumb in his direction. "But don't say I didn't warn you. And please don't tell Dad you let a murderer sleep in your house."

His fists clenched at his side. He wanted to defend himself in the best way he knew how, but his body still ached from the night before, and he didn't want to start a fight in Brooklyn's kitchen. She didn't deserve two jacked-up guys fighting for the top dog position. He'd seen this enough in prison to know what was about to happen, if he allowed it. He took a breath and held it, instead.

"I should be going." He adjusted the duffel on his shoulder. "Um, did you move my bike?"

"I couldn't leave it by the road."

"That's a pretty heavy bike for you to lift. I left it laying on the ground." He had to admit she impressed him. He didn't think someone her size would be able to get the bike on its tires. Her hands were small like the rest of her. She only came up to his collarbone, but she was strong and determined. Still the same Brooklyn.

"I was a nurse. I'm used to moving dead weight around." She shot Brad a death glare. Her glance had to have a double meaning. "Besides, what if someone tried to take it?" She didn't wait for an answer. "I walked it down the drive. I don't think you can ride it, though. Something was dragging on the ground." She grabbed a spatula from a drawer and worked the eggs.

"I've got some duct tape in the truck," Brad said. "Tape it

up and get out of here, Ransom. You aren't welcome near my family."

"Brad, for God's sake, shut up." She turned to him. "I'm sorry, Caleb. Don't listen to him. He was just leaving."

Caleb bit the inside of his cheek to keep from smiling.

Brad swiped the metal coffee mug that was on the table. "Have him out of here within the hour before the whole town starts talking." He left without another word. The door closed with a loud thud.

"I'm sorry about that." Brooklyn dropped into a chair and hung her head. The sunlight caught the golds in her hair that drifted over her face. She was always beautiful. She had snagged his heart when they were teens and his family lived on the edge of the alpaca farm. That house was gone now. He never found out why it had been neglected. Eventually, the elements had had their way with her. Someone had torn it down. The land stood empty, stretching all the way to the rolling hills.

"There's no need to be sorry. I'm used to the angry distrust of others." He stole a glance at the eggs. His stomach growled. He hoped she couldn't hear that.

She stared straight at him. "You still look pretty banged up. You scared me when you collapsed. How are you feeling?"

"I'll be okay." The pain had lulled to a dull throb now. If he didn't breathe too deeply, his ribs didn't hurt at all. "How did I get to the bedroom? I'm pretty sure you didn't carry me." He put the duffel down and tried not to grimace with the movement. He didn't want her to tend to him. He owed her enough already, especially for standing up to her brother on his behalf.

"You walked. Well, it was more like you leaned on me, and I walked you. You don't remember that?"

That explained a few things, but not everything. "Vaguely.

I wasn't in my clothes. Did you get me like that?" A memory tapped him on the shoulder. Brooklyn had managed to take his clothes off a few times—a lifetime ago. Did those memories ever stop her in her tracks, stealing her breath but also warming a smile on her lips? Or was that just him?

"You couldn't sleep in those bloody clothes. I threw out your shirt. There was no saving it. I washed your jeans. Are you sure you're okay?" She busied herself with filling the tea kettle.

She had done his laundry and retrieved his bike from the road too. He couldn't remember the last time someone did so many nice things for him in the same twelve hours. "Thanks for helping me out. I think I was more exhausted than injured at that point. It had been a very long day."

He had been driving for hours and hadn't eaten most of the day. He had needed to get to Candlewood Falls before the day ended. He never missed the anniversary of his mother's death. He would drive from wherever he was holed up to bring flowers to her grave and sit with her awhile, talking. She had always made time for him, listening to anything he wanted to talk about even when he was in jail. Working on no sleep to get to her gravesite was the least he could do for his mother.

"Well, if nothing else eat something before you go. I mean, you're still going, right?" She moved to the stove and scooped eggs onto a plate. The tea kettle whistled through the room and rattled his head.

"I think that's what your brother wants."

She placed the plate on the table. "Eat. I don't care what my brother wants. I am tired of caring about what other people want." She leaned against the counter and crossed her arms over her chest.

She could stop time with her long hair, high cheekbones, and petite frame. She had always been pretty, but her beauty had matured since he saw her last. Her eyes were no longer wide with innocence. He could suspect the dark circles were from her being up all night taking care of him, but something told him, maybe the mature knowing that had settled in her gaze, or better yet the shotgun she had come to the door with, that even Brooklyn had seen the tougher side of life.

"I can agree with not caring about what other people want, but I don't remember you being that way." The smell of the eggs in front of him and the bread in the toaster taunted his empty stomach.

He sat at the table, wanting to prolong this visit after all. Finding Brooklyn here was a nice surprise and with a motorcycle in no condition to drive, his hurry to leave could wait until after breakfast.

"Yeah, well, things have changed."

He was right then. She had been through some tough times. The idea of her struggling made his heart hurt. He never would've wanted that for her and hoped he didn't hold much of the blame.

"When did you come back to Candlewood Falls?" He stabbed at the food with a fork and kept his gaze on the plate. The eggs were warm and buttery with a hint of salt. She had added mushrooms and spinach. The best damn eggs he'd had in a long time.

She poured tea into one mug and coffee into another for him. She took the seat opposite his, holding the mug in front of her like a shield. "About six months ago. My husband and I split up."

"I'm sorry to hear that." He mopped the egg up with his bread. He tried to control himself from licking the plate. He wondered what had happened that would have her husband leaving. Brooklyn had a lot to offer. Or least she had when he knew her well. She was kind when others were cruel. She always wanted to save a stray cat or let a spider back out into

17

nature. She could pull laughter out of him at times when it seemed like he might never laugh again. Maybe the husband hadn't appreciated her honesty. "Your ex-husband is pretty stupid if he let you go."

Her hand fluttered by her neck. "Thank you. That's nice of you to say. But believe me, I'm not sorry the marriage ended. It was time. Why are you in town? You don't live here. I would've seen you, if you did."

Candlewood Falls was a small town, but not so small you bumped into everyone every day. Did that mean that she had been checking for him? That idea filled his chest with something pleasing. *Don't go getting sentimental. It causes trouble.* He rubbed his fist into his sternum until the sensation went away.

"I was passing through." He had foolishly thought it would be okay to stop at Murphy's just one time. He had been exhausted like he had said. He had only wanted an hour before he had to begin the ride to the next town with no name where he would check in to another nameless motel and begin the search for a job. He should never have stopped no matter how tired or lonely he might have been. If he had left the cemetery and drove out of town unnoticed, whoever had followed him and nearly killed him would never have seen him.

He was certain he had been followed, but he hadn't noticed anyone in Murphy's who would still want him dead. Sure, there were plenty of people in this town who still hated him, Brad Wilde being one of them. He had chosen a table in the dark corner, and he sat with his back to the wall so he could watch the door. And still had missed an emissary.

"Passing through to where? Is it someplace far from here?" Her voice dragged him back to her bright kitchen and away from the dark interior of his thoughts.

"Why? Are you looking for a new place to live?" He

smirked at his own stupid joke, but Brooklyn's face stayed impassive.

She pushed out of the chair and went to the window. "Maybe. I don't know where I belong anymore. I'm trying to figure it out, anyway."

He hadn't expected such an honest answer, but he should from her. He could relate. He had lost everything, including his freedom for two years. Since his time in prison, he didn't belong anywhere. He couldn't put down roots because eventually people wanted to know about his past. That was not a story he ever shared.

"Thank you for breakfast and for a place to sleep. I need to get out of here and see if my bike can be fixed." He needed some air too. Being near Brooklyn and getting dangerously close to the feelings that have choked him for years was more than he could take in two days. He just wanted to get on his bike and drive until the place and the woman that haunted him were miles behind him.

She flinched at his sudden movement from the table. "Oh. Are you sure? Do you want to call a tow truck or something?"

"No, thanks. I can probably get it to work." He sure as hell hoped he could. At least work well enough to get him to the next town. Then he could find a mechanic who knew more than he did.

"Take care of yourself, Caleb." She smoothed her hands over her legs.

"You too." He averted his gaze and grabbed his duffel. The eggs sat like lead in his stomach. He forced himself not to look back when the screen door slapped shut behind him.

Brooklyn was a part of his past, a past that didn't need to be remembered. He hadn't killed SJ Wilde, but this town didn't believe him. Even if Brooklyn was being kind, or maybe thought he actually was innocent, it didn't matter. He didn't belong here.

His motorcycle leaning against the porch railing stopped him short. "Shit."

He wasn't going anywhere.

For a while.

CHAPTER THREE

B rooklyn needed caffeine. The tea she had this morning wasn't cutting it. Not after the night she had. She never slept well anymore. Not since the attack which was almost a year ago. But after Caleb arrived, startling her beyond recognition, and needing medical attention, sleep had taken its toys and gone home. That's what had her pushing his very heavy motorcycle up the driveway in the rain and doing his laundry. Well, she had some clothes that needed laundering too. Adding his jeans wasn't a big deal.

She pulled on the door of the Green Bean. A nutty and caramelized smell enveloped the shop with its small tables and glass case of goodies. Most of the tables were filled with people deep in conversation, paying no attention to her. She preferred to blend in these days. She had been told after her attack, it had been random, but she still wondered what it had been about her that had attracted the attacker. He must've noticed something. She didn't want to be noticed by strangers, which was one of the reasons she had returned to Candlewood Falls. Most people in town knew her and who her family was.

She inhaled the nutty coffee smell. Green Bean had the best bold brew anywhere. She didn't have the heart to tell her family who offered coffee at Wilde Orchard's bakery that Green Bean's coffee was better. The pastries were fantastic; no one could beat the apple cider donuts they made right on the premises, but the coffee...not so much.

The last place she wanted to be this morning, anyway, was the orchard even if she had loved the coffee there. She didn't want to run into Brad again who could be anywhere on the property, barking orders at his workers. She was also likely to run into her father who made an appearance regularly since he was part owner. She wasn't sure she could look her dad in the eye, even at her age, and omit the fact Caleb Ransom spent the night in the extra bedroom. Her father still suspected Caleb as the killer for his brother. She didn't blame him. SJ's death was unnecessary. It stood to reason her father would want a reason for it, and Caleb was a good one.

She slid into line and ordered a large black coffee with a blueberry muffin on the side. A buzz of whispers bounced around as if someone had disturbed a hornet's nest. The words *break-in* and *attacked* made goosebumps pop out on her skin. She couldn't bear the idea that someone's home had been broken into, and certainly not in Candlewood Falls. That kind of thing didn't happen here. She hurried to the fixings bar, trying to get away from any more talk of a robbery. The Green Bean was suddenly too hot.

"Did you hear the news?" The female voice scratched and dented with years of use startled her.

She turned to find Weezer River standing beside her, pouring milk into her own coffee. "Good morning, Weezer. What news is that?" The sugar packet slipped from her fingers and landed in the coffee, packaging and all. She fished it out with a wooden stirrer and cursed her nerves.

Weezer River was a permanent fixture in Candlewood

Falls and the owner of Rivers Edge winery that ran behind the Wilde Orchard. Weezer knew where all the secrets were buried and wasn't afraid to dig them up. But Brooklyn knew a secret about Weezer. She had a heart.

"Someone broke into old lady Holloway's last night. They stole jewelry and money and smacked her around. I'm surprised you didn't hear something, or one of those filthy alpacas didn't scream their heads off."

Her grandmother's alpacas were not dirty. In fact, the alpacas were quite clean and didn't smell. She couldn't say the same for Weezer. A trail of disinfectant and muscle cream drifted off her like a thick fog. The other secret not many knew about Weezer was she actually liked the alpacas. Especially Alpacino. Alpacino often got loose because of the broken fence Brooklyn would need to fix and ended up at the winery.

"I hadn't heard about any break-in. Is she okay?" Other than the conversations she had bumped into right here at the Green Bean. Her hands shook as she stirred the milk into the coffee. Mrs. Holloway lived next door to her, more than fifteen acres away, but it wouldn't be hard for someone to jump the fence and run straight to Cordy's house. Brooklyn could've been the one last night who had been assaulted and robbed.

The plastic lid slipped out of her still trembling hand. Her fingers jerked and scraped the lid in a motion to grab it before it hit the floor. The cup fell over with a plop. Milk and coffee poured over the fixing bar and splashed on the floor, hitting her boots and Weezer's sneakers.

"What is the matter with you? Have you been drinking this morning? Honestly." Weezer ripped napkins from the metal holder and blotted her shoes.

A young woman with a blond braid running down her back and wearing a Green Bean apron hurried over with towels. "It's okay. We'll get you another one," she said with a sympathetic smile that lit up a dimple in her cheek.

The barista's words didn't register at first. Even the messy scene in front of her confused her brain like a good jigsaw puzzle. "I'm sorry. I don't know what happened." But she did. The talk of a robbery and an attack had sent her nerves over the edge. It probably had to do with the lack of sleep and Caleb's arrival. He had turned her world on its head, standing at her door unexpectedly. She had missed him and hadn't even known it until last night.

"You're a klutz," Weezer said and leaned in. "I think I know what has you frazzled this morning. So, let me give you a piece of advice; don't give these people anything else to gossip about. You've already handed them a plateful when you came back." Weezer's breath was hot and smelled of coffee. She tossed her napkins in the garbage with a huff and stalked out, her fur coat floating in the wind behind her.

She had no idea what Weezer was talking about. People couldn't possibly care about her spilled coffee, but when she looked around many of the faces were turned in her direction. Their mouths hung open like a barn door on broken hinges. Heat ran up her neck. Word was already out that Caleb had been at her house. Gossip in this town moved faster than an electric fire.

"It's just coffee, people." She tried to laugh off her blunder.

"I heard it was more than that," someone said just loud enough to be heard over the sounds of the coffee shop.

"What did you say?" Though she wasn't entirely sure who had said it. The customers had turned back to their conversations as if nothing had happened, forgetting she was even there.

No one responded. The pretty barista returned with a new to-go cup of hot black coffee.

"Thank you." She took the cup, but she no longer wanted it. She certainly didn't need it. Her adrenaline pumped like a well-oiled machine after learning Mrs. Holloway had been attacked. Nowhere was safe. She had hoped if she came home, things would change. She wouldn't be frightened all the time. But nothing had changed. She was still the same. Just as Caleb had said, but not in the way he had meant.

She pushed outside into the warm fall afternoon thick with humidity and aggressive bees not ready to accept their time left was numbered. She tugged on the collar of her sweater that seemed like a good idea this morning when the day was still damp with a chill. She dumped the coffee into the garbage and searched for her keys in her purse. She wanted to be anywhere but on Main Street where visitors and residents moved from shop to shop.

Candlewood Falls was a quaint and historic town on the west side of New Jersey with a walking bridge on Main Street that offered a picturesque view of the old red mill. It was the kind of town families came for the day to visit the orchard where they could pick apples or bring a picnic lunch and sit in the gazebo, watching people come and go. Or where women groups gathered to sip wine and shop in the locally owned stores on Main Street. Candlewood Falls was in her blood. She had stayed away too long. Now she couldn't imagine waking up anywhere else and had no immediate intentions of leaving the alpaca farm. She loved those animals and loved living with her grandmother. Brooklyn only wished that a crime hadn't been committed right next door to her house.

A magnetic pull grabbed her gaze and directed it across the street to Hafrey's Garage. Or maybe it had been the voices on the wind that had drawn her out of her own thoughts.

Jameson, the garage's owner, stood beside a man, a tall man

with a mop of black hair and wearing a leather biker's jacket. Jameson's arms moved as he spoke, directing a conversation she couldn't hear, but wished she could. A look of confusion passed over the chiseled face of this dangerously handsome man. The man who had shown up at her doorstep late at night and injured.

That man had no way out of town by the looks of his motorcycle leaning against the garage and the tight set of his jaw. Caleb Ransom was sticking around, at least for a short time. A tingle ran down her spine, but she shook it off. His arrival on her doorstep had meant nothing. The past must stay in the past.

"You bent your fork and handlebars." Jameson Hafrey scratched the back of his head with a hand covered in grease. "Did a deer run out into the road and cut you off?"

"Something like that. The side of the bike looks like I took a cheese grater to it." So did the side of his torso. Every time he shifted, his shirt rubbed against the road rash and sent waves of pain up and down his skin. "Can you fix it?"

"Sure, I can. But it's going to take me a week or two. I've got to order the parts for the broken mirrors and control lever. The fuel tanks don't come painted. If you want that color black again, I'll need a couple of days for that too."

His motorcycle was his only possession worth anything. He didn't care much for things because objects could be replaced and taken away at a moment's notice. But his motorcycle had been the one thing that helped him get from place to place. When he rode her, he could put distance between him and the memories that chased him all the time.

"Fine. Do what you need to." He didn't have much choice except to allow Jameson to fix the bike. It would be easier than pushing it all the way to the next town. Problem was he would be stuck in Candlewood Falls.

Main Street hadn't changed much over the years. The store fronts were still there, lined up like soldiers in a row. Some of the shops had changed. Something called Witchy Woman hadn't always been there. He had no idea what kind of a store that was. Someone named Vivian owned the hair salon based on the sign. People still walked in laughing groups up and down the street or stood on the walking bridge taking pictures of the waterfall. It was all familiar and foreign at the same time. An unease rested in his gut. He didn't belong here, wasn't wanted here, and couldn't hide here either.

"You know, you're lucky you weren't hurt worse. Were you wearing that leather jacket?" Jameson's voice pulled his attention away from the passersby.

"I was." For all the good it did. He hadn't had it zipped, which had been stupid in the rain.

"Guess someone was watching out for you."

He didn't believe in guardian angels or any of that. He sure as hell didn't believe in God because he had prayed a million times for God to help him out of the jam he was in when he got arrested. God never answered.

"Maybe," he said. He liked to think his mother checked in on him from time to time from her spot in Heaven or wherever she went. Her stubborn persistence had been the one thing that got him out of jail. She hadn't quit until she had proved he was innocent. And he was.

"I'll need a number where I can reach you." Jameson pulled a pen from his shirt pocket.

He gave Jameson his cell number. He had been real lucky his phone hadn't been demolished in the crash like his bike. It only suffered a few scratches. He couldn't afford to buy a new phone at the moment. "Does the B and B still rent out rooms?"

"The one over at the Wilde Orchard? Not at the moment. It's sitting pretty quiet over there. Lacey Wilde had cancer."

"Wow. Sorry to hear that. Does anyone rent out a room?" He could take a driving service to another town. Hell, he could cross the state line into Pennsylvania and find a bed and breakfast in New Hope without much effort, but he wanted to be nearby in case his bike was done early. The fewer days spent in Candlewood Falls the better.

"I don't know." Jameson averted his gaze and went back to staring at the bike as if it would show him something new.

"I get it." No one would rent a room to him, if there was even a room to be had in this town.

"I'll be in touch." Jameson stuck out his hand.

He stared for a minute before shaking. Jameson had a job to do and could explain to the haters about taking business from a man like him. Money was money, after all. But recommend a place for him to stay? No, the people of this town would never forgive Jameson for an indiscretion like that one.

With the rest of the day stretching out before him like an intrusive yawn, he turned to go. He had no idea where. He couldn't roam around the streets all week until his bike was ready. Maybe he could slip into that coffee shop for a couple of hours and search the internet for a place to rent for the week. He would be sure to stay out of the bar. He would like to find somewhere to hole up before dark when everyone went home to their families and their private lives and Main Street was empty. Whoever had followed him last night might still be looking for him. A dark street would be a good place to ambush someone. Maybe New Hope was a better option after all.

"Caleb?" Brooklyn stood on the sidewalk with her hand

shielding her eyes from the midmorning sun. She crossed the street and met him halfway.

"Hey. What brings you into town?" The question was dumb, but he wasn't exactly sure what to say to her. He had left abruptly this morning never expecting to see her again. He really appreciated what she had done for him, but he didn't want her to face trouble because of him. Anyone watching them would draw the wrong conclusions.

"I was running some errands."

A car sped past and honked at them. "Maybe we should get out of the road." He led her back to the safety of the sidewalk. He hadn't meant to touch her, but his hand went to her low back as if it belonged there. As if it remembered all on its own, she had once belonged to him.

"How's the bike?" She smiled and shifted her purse on her shoulder. At least she hadn't flinched at his touch.

"Pretty messed up. It's going to take a couple of weeks to get fixed." He stole a glance over his shoulder at Jameson. The garage swallowed up his bike like a great white finding food. What this town would do to him if he weren't careful.

"I'm sorry to hear that. What are you going to do?" She fished out her phone and checked the screen, but didn't scroll, as if she were checking the time. Was she meeting someone or just trying to avoid eye contact?

"Find a place to stay for the time being. You don't happen to know anyone with a room to rent, do you?" He needed a room from someone who had moved into Candlewood Falls after he left, or at the very least someone who wasn't completely connected to the Wildes.

"You're going to stay in town?" She tucked her phone back in her purse and stared at him with wide eyes.

"It's easier than catching a ride somewhere else. Everything's so spread out in this county. I want to be nearby when Jameson is done and not thirty minutes or more away."

He should've asked Jameson if he could sleep on the garage floor.

She ran her fingers along the side of her neck. "Well, Cordy won't be home for a few more weeks. You could stay with me. I wouldn't mind the company." She pushed her hair away from her face with a trembling hand.

"Are you okay?" He reached for her but stopped. She wouldn't want comfort from the man her family suspected had caused so much pain. Her family had come between them after he had gone to prison. She had visited him once or twice, but without warning, she had stopped coming and stopped answering his letters.

"Of course. I'm fine. Why wouldn't I be?" She gripped the strap of that purse with both hands.

She wasn't a very good liar. Her gaze bounced around, avoiding his. Even if she wasn't gripping her bag with a white-knuckled fist, her teeth did a number on her bottom lip. Something had this woman worked up, and he could probably guess what it was.

"That's generous, but you don't have to offer me a place to stay. I understand."

"I don't think you do, actually." She squared her shoulders and tilted up her chin.

"What's your family going to say when they find out I'm sleeping down the hall from you?" He had slept in her bed once, but that had been a lifetime ago. He hadn't had a lot to offer her back then, but after getting arrested, he had nothing for a woman like Brooklyn who deserved everything.

"I don't care what my family says. I barely speak to my cousins. And as for my father and my brother, they can just deal with it. I know we haven't kept in touch, but can't we be friends?"

"I'm not sure that's a good idea. I bring a lot of baggage you don't need." He would love to pick up where they had left off if only as friends. He had thought of her often wondering how she was and what she was doing.

"Well, how about I don't want to be alone at the farm right now. Someone broke into Mrs. Holloway's house. She lives next door."

"You've got that big shotgun." He was grateful she hadn't blown his head off with it.

"It wasn't loaded, and I don't know how to use it."

"You came to the door with an unloaded gun? Smart and at the same time, keep that secret to yourself. You don't want anyone using that gun against you."

"Yesterday I would've said, it's Candlewood Falls. No one is going to hurt me, but if someone can beat up poor Mrs. Holloway, you're right about the gun. I really would like the company. What do you say? Rent the room from me."

"I don't know." They were both taking a huge risk by having his presence at the farm. He had been desperate last night, but now he could handle his injuries. He wasn't sure he was up for having to deal with her brother or her father.

"You won't have to deal with the alpacas. I have a helper for that, Malinda. I'll make sure to overcharge you, if you want." Her smile hesitated across her face as if she were waiting for him to understand her joke. When he laughed, she followed and that warm spot from this morning returned to his chest. He tried to rub it away again.

"I wouldn't want to take away your chance to overcharge a tenant. You have a deal, but I don't mind helping around the farm. I need to stay busy." He was probably going to regret this decision for her as much as for himself. But time with Brooklyn had always struck him the way a walk into the light does after coming out of the dark.

"Great. Do you want a ride back to the house? I'm parked around the corner."

"Caleb Ransom, don't move."

He spun at the authoritarian tone shouting at him. It was a knee-jerk reaction from his time in prison. A short stocky man with aviator sunglasses and a scowl barreled in their direction. The blue uniform and gun belt made his presence looming, but even without those things, this man would have made Caleb cross the street to avoid confrontation like staying out of the way of an angry bucking horse. Officer Zahn Vetter had hated him most of his life.

Brooklyn stared at him with confusion in her eyes and a raised brow. He didn't understand what was happening either, but he was about to find out.

"Officer Vetter, I see you haven't retired yet." He willed his heart to slow and his breathing to stay even. He had done nothing wrong. Vetter had no reason to start with him, but that didn't mean he wouldn't. Vetter had been the officer to arrest him when SJ Wilde was murdered. Vetter had painted a slanted version of what he really had walked up on that night, and like a rabid dog, Vetter didn't stop until Caleb was behind bars.

"I get a break-in and an assault in one night, and imagine my surprise when I found out that you were back in town. Where were you last night?" Vetter stopped inches from him and raised his glasses. His black eyes were void of emotion.

"How did you know I was back in town?" He didn't have to tell Vetter where he was. He knew his rights. But he also knew how easy it was for the police to make the facts fit the way they wanted them to.

"It's Candlewood Falls. I have eyes and ears everywhere. Where did you go after you left Murphy's last night?" Vetter fisted his hands on his hips.

"Maybe the question should be who played chicken with him on the road last night and made him spin out? He could've died." Brooklyn inserted herself between him and

Officer Vetter. She tilted up her chin and fisted her hands on her hips.

"Brooklyn, it's okay." He stepped around her with his heart in his throat. What she had just done had been brave and foolish at the same time. She didn't need to be tied to him. Nothing good would come of it.

Vetter tugged on the end of his nose. "Ransom, did someone drive recklessly, causing you to crash? Would you like to fill out a report?" He put his hands on his gun belt and tapped his foot.

"No, thanks. It's all good. I'm going to have my bike fixed and then I'm out of your town." He held his hands up.

"I still want to know where you were last night between the hours of eleven and midnight."

He wasn't completely sure what time he had left the bar. It might've been closer to ten thirty. The drive out of town didn't take long, but he wasn't sure how long he was lying on the side of the road before he could get up. He had also struggled to make it to Cordy's farm. The rain and the dark had turned him around. Probably the hit to the head too. He had his helmet on, but its open face was what caused the bloody nose and his swollen eye. He did look as if he had been in a fight last night.

"He was with me." Brooklyn crossed her arms over her chest.

"Is that what you want your father or your uncle Huck to know?" Vetter dropped his sunglasses to the edge of his nose and eyed her over the frame.

"Who I spend my time with is no one's business including my father and certainly not my uncle's. Is that all? I need to get back to my farm."

"Were you with her, Ransom?"

He didn't know what Brooklyn was trying to do. If it got out that he hadn't shown up to her house until after midnight, which is what he was almost certain of because of the clock on the mantel in her living room, she would get into trouble. He didn't want her to lie for him. She was too good to get dragged into his crap.

Brooklyn stared at him with wide eyes.

He could tell the truth. He'd probably get arrested just because Vetter had no other suspects like last time. He wouldn't need that room to rent because the jail cell would come free of charge with three meals a day too. Or he could make a run for it. Forget his bike. He could buy another one in another town. A town without the name Candlewood Falls on the welcome sign.

"Yeah, Vetter. I was with her all night."

CHAPTER FOUR

B rooklyn turned onto the long driveway up to the alpaca farm. The driveway was mostly dirt and gravel, but it was lined with mature Bradford pear trees that were beautiful spring, summer, and fall. This time of year, their bright-orange leaves stretched high into the sky and wide to the sides, welcoming her back to the farm each and every time. As a kid, she would grab a book and sit in their shade for hours until her grandmother found her. They were her favorite landscaping tree.

She navigated the last of the dips and bumps and hit the brakes, knocking her and Caleb forward in their seats. He tossed her a sideways glance.

"I don't have to stay," he said.

"My father has nothing to say about this farm. This is Cordy's farm, and I'm sure she would be happy to have you." She would have to call Cordy before someone in town got to her first. If one of the ladies from her knitting club had heard about Caleb, they would interrupt her vacation without a second thought. Cordy should hear from her that they had an unusual guest.

She had hoped for more time to talk to her father about what she had said to Officer Vetter, but Vetter had probably called her uncle Huck before she and Caleb had even driven away. Once Uncle Huck found out she was Caleb's alibi, he wouldn't waste a second to call her dad. Uncle Huck never missed an opportunity to fight with her father. They might be brothers, but they weren't family.

Her father leaned against the back of his dirty pickup. He wore his hair a little longer these days. Even in his fifties her father had most of his hair, though more gray than brown now. His salt-and-pepper beard traveled onto his neck because he couldn't be bothered to trim it. His black button-down shirt hung over his faded jeans. His boots were dust covered much like his truck. Her mother had once thought Dad looked like a young Sean Connery. That was before he decided to live off the land and give up modern conveniences. He was a handsome man because of the lines around his eyes and his easy smile. But mostly because he was filled with love for her and Brad. Except right now. Now he narrowed those blue eyes and the corner of his mouth had dropped. He was expecting an answer.

"Maybe you should've asked Cordy if she minded that I stayed before you took on Vetter." His smile touched his eyes. "You're pretty tough, you know that?"

"Sometimes." Though the queasiness in her stomach said otherwise. She never wanted her father to be mad at her, even at her age. "Let me handle my father. You can wait here." She opened the door on a long breath.

"Gladly." He threw a hand up and looked out the side window.

She pushed out of the car and marched over to the man who made her feel safe and loved her whole life. He had played imaginary games with her when she was little and her mother had left for the glitz and glamour she had craved instead of a simple life on an apple orchard. Dad had come to all her school events despite his doubts about public schools even in New Jersey where the schools were second to none.

Now he only came over when he had something important to discuss. He hated the cell phone and had only agreed to own one because she had begged him to have a phone for emergencies. He kept it off most of the time because he didn't like being tracked.

"What's up, Dad?" The gravel crunched under her shoes. The alpacas wandered over to the edge of the barn as if they could sense the tension in the air. Lucy gave a short squeal but turned and waddled back inside.

She and Brad had spent their early years living in a house with normal lives like most people. But one day her father started squirreling away canned foods and water. Her mother didn't protest much at first. She had believed Silas had a new hobby and eventually he'd give up that quest. Instead, he built a cabin in the woods. The property belonged to the Wilde family which meant he didn't have to ask for permission other than a short conversation with his father Skip. Silas Wilde was a man of few words. She and Brad weren't more than twelve when Silas told his wife they would be moving into that cabin. He would allow the children to attend the school; he wouldn't cut his ties with the orchard, but he needed space and peace and quiet. Her mother divorced her father instead.

"What do you think you're doing?" He twisted a long piece of hay between his fingers.

"I'm standing in the driveway speaking with my father."

"You know what I mean. How did you get tangled up with him?" Dad spit out the last word.

"Did Uncle Huck call you? Or was it Brad? Did he tell on me?" She didn't need anyone deciding what was right for her.

She would make that decision. Ever since the attack, someone was trying to tell her how to act and what to do.

"Does it matter how I know? I know. The whole town knows."

"Since when do you care what the people of this town think? That's not exactly your style." If he had given one ounce of caring, she wouldn't have grown up in a cabin she couldn't invite her friends to because they had to pee in the outhouse. She had to entertain friends on the orchard. She never blamed her father for his choices, but they weren't always easy to live with. He should give her a little slack where her choices were concerned.

"That boy killed my brother. Now, I know SJ had some problems." He put his hands up in surrender. The piece of hay tumbled to the ground. "He was bound to end up dead in an alley one way or another, but that don't give someone the right to decide when that time was going to be. I don't want you messing with him, Brooklyn. He's no good. No good for you. No good for our family."

"He was exonerated. He didn't kill Uncle SJ." She glanced over her shoulder. Caleb sat slouched in the front seat. The man she had known all those years ago couldn't have been a killer, but he had had a temper that landed him in more than one fight. The argument with her uncle that dreaded night could've escalated to a dangerous level, but Caleb had always maintained he had walked up on SJ already on the ground, bleeding and out cold.

"He was let out on a technicality. That's not the same thing. I don't want him staying with you. It's not safe," Dad said.

"He needs a place to stay until his motorcycle is fixed. Since Cordy is away, I thought the company would be nice. I don't want to be alone after what happened to Mrs. Holloway. You can understand that, can't you?"

Her father pressed his lips together in a thin line. She could only tell because of the twitch of his facial hair. Her father was well aware of what had happened to her last year. For the first time in a long time, he had left Candlewood Falls to come be by her side while she lay curled up in a ball in the hospital. He hated the crowded city she lived in, but he had come for her.

"You can come stay with me until Cordy comes back."

"No, thanks. My days of roughing it in the cabin are over." The cabin had one bedroom, a living area, and a loft. If she stood in the center of the cabin, she could almost extend both arms and touch two walls. When they were kids, she and Brad had to share the bedroom while Dad slept in the loft.

She needed space now. Surely, he was someone who understood the need for space. She wished she didn't have to spell it out for him, but anything too small only made her throat close and her body break out in a sweat.

"Then stay with Brad or on the orchard. At least there you won't be alone. Grandpa will give you a room in his house."

"I don't want to stay with Brad or Grandpa. I like it here. I like helping out with the alpacas. I don't want to run away. I just want a little company." She was tired of running. She was also tired of being afraid, but she hadn't completely worked that out. At least at the farm, she had some peace. In that regard, she was a lot like her dad. The space and the rolling hills soothed her soul. The farm was her safe haven. The alpacas were good company during the day. The nights she hadn't come to terms with yet.

"Then I'll stay with you."

"Yeah, right. You'll last about a day before you'll want to go back up your mountain. You could barely handle coming to me last year."

"But I did it."

"And I love you for it." She had been lucky to have a dad like him even with all his eccentricities. She had known girls growing up whose fathers were rich and lived in big houses with every luxury, but acted as if their little girls didn't exist. She wouldn't trade her dad for any man like that.

"He's a killer." His words held less conviction than before. She had secretly believed her father doubted Caleb had been the one. Dad knew things about Uncle SJ he had never revealed and probably never would.

"Cordy doesn't think he's a killer, and neither do I." At least she didn't want to believe it. But maybe her judgment was all wrong. Caleb wasn't the same person she knew before. She certainly wasn't. And after her attack, she didn't know who her husband had been either. She had expected him to be there for her, be her rock, but he couldn't handle what had happened. He had pulled away from her as if the sight of her made him sick.

"You're making a mistake, Cheeks." The use of her child-hood nickname caught her off guard. The ground shifted under her. "Don't say I didn't warn you." He arched a brow.

She wanted to protest, but Caleb limped down the driveway as fast as his injuries would allow. Her father would see his swollen eye and bruised face and assume Caleb had gotten into a fight. "Mr. Wilde, can I talk to you for a second?"

"I've got nothing to say to you, son. But let it be known, I don't want you here. I disagree with my daughter's choice, but she's a grown woman. I can't stop her. I just wish she'd be less stubborn and listen to me." Her father hitched his leg into the truck and kicked the engine over. He pulled away, kicking up dirt without another look in their direction.

Her heart sunk. "I'm sorry. My family can be difficult." She couldn't wait for Cordy to return from her vacation and life on the farm could get back to normal. Maybe Cordy could have a talk with her father. Her grandmother and father had stayed close all these years. Cordy and her dad shared Patricia Sutter's disapproval of them. Patricia, Cordy's daughter and Silas's wife, had no patience for dirt under her fingernails, the smell of hay clinging to her clothes, a husband who planned for the end of the world, or a mother who owned alpacas.

Unfortunately, her mother also had no patience for her children. Patricia had left her and Brad with barely more than a look back. In no time at all, Patricia had found another man who could buy her nice things and give her a big, expensive house to live in. She had tried her mother's world for a short time while she had been married, but that life fit like a collar choking off the air flow. She belonged in Candlewood Falls where she could breathe.

"I can call for a cab or a driving service. You don't need this aggravation," Caleb said.

"You're staying, And that's that." She turned on her heel and hoped he would follow. She really did want the company. Maybe Caleb was a bad choice to share the house with while she was alone and frightened someone would break into her home, but something inside her made her think Caleb would keep her safe. Maybe it was because Cordy would never have been fooled by Caleb. She always trusted Cordy.

She stopped just inside the front door. Caleb's footsteps pounded the wood planks of the porch and came up on her heels. His breath was labored, probably from all the discomfort he was in. The heat rolled off him, standing so close to her, and brought with it a hint of his earthy scent.

"Thank you," he said on a whisper.

"Of course." She did have a question that had never been answered and it wouldn't be today, if ever, because she didn't know if she should voice it. If Caleb hadn't killed Uncle SJ, then who had?

With the alpacas fed and settling down in their barn for the night, Brooklyn wanted to go next door to visit Mrs. Holloway. She pulled Cordy's banana bread out of the oven and let it cool on the wire rack. The comforting smell of banana, brown sugar and cinnamon filled the room, but did nothing to ease the tension in her neck. The whole day she worried about who might have hurt Mrs. Holloway and would they be back for more.

She grabbed plastic wrap from the drawer and hoped the dessert might cheer Mrs. Holloway up a little. But she knew deep down, after being brutalized and made vulnerable by a complete stranger, something as insignificant as banana bread wouldn't be able to offer a sense of security or an explanation. The gesture was simply a way to let Mrs. H know she wasn't alone.

Brooklyn glanced out the window over the sink. The days had receded like an old man's hairline as autumn took up residence in Candlewood Falls, which meant the land between the farm and Mrs. H's place was a vast wasteland unpenetrated by light. The dark was thick and full, suffocating even. She forced a deep breath into her lungs and wrapped the banana bread in the plastic wrap. She could drive over. Nobody would think anything of that. The grass was probably damp with dew and maybe even still wet from the rain the other night, or she could put one of the alpacas on a leash and walk over. But if a fox was out there, she'd have some trouble. Driving would have to be the way, because she wasn't walking alone. Not at night.

Caleb strolled into the kitchen in his stocking feet and snatched an apple from the bowl on the table. He tossed it in the air before wiping it on his tight-fitting shirt that outlined the muscles in his arms and plunged his teeth into the shiny red skin. The apple snapped open and juice ran down his chin. "Your orchard grows the best apples," he said between bites.

"We think so." She scratched at the scar on her neck from her incident last year. It didn't itch the way it had when it first healed and a scab had formed. The skin was raised, but the pink had faded. When she saw herself in the mirror, she almost didn't notice it. "Hey, um, if you aren't doing anything, would you consider going next door with me? I wanted to bring the banana bread to Mrs. Holloway and see how she's doing."

She held her breath.

He stared at her for a second, his hand with the apple paused in midair by his mouth. "I can't."

"Do you have plans?"

"I can't be seen over there. I don't need to give Vetter any possible piece of information that could link me to the crime scene." He tossed the remainder of the apple in the garbage.

"But how is going next door with me giving him a way to link you to the crime? You said you didn't do it, then you didn't do it."

"You really believe it's that easy. Even after what happened to me? How naive are you? What I say doesn't matter, not if he can produce enough evidence to say the opposite. People like you always believe things will work out. Things don't work out for people like me."

"Caleb, I think you're overreacting."

"I'm not going with you. Being your escort isn't part of the room rental agreement. We aren't friends anymore. We don't socialize. That woman doesn't know me anyway. She wouldn't want me knocking on her door with some dessert." A sneer twisted its way around his voice like a rattlesnake. He stormed out of the room. The slamming of the bedroom door punctuated his exit.

She placed her hands on the cool counter and took a steadying breath. She did not understand where that outburst had come from. Just a few hours ago, he had thanked her for sticking up for him with her father. Now, he lost it when she had only asked a simple question? She didn't deserve a response like that.

She marched down the hall and banged on the bedroom door. "Caleb, open up. I think we need to talk."

Silence on the other end, but then shuffling and the knob turned. He pulled open the door and stared at her. "There isn't anything to talk about."

"What just happened in there? I asked you to come next door with me and you bit my head off."

"You believe everything will always work out because for you it does. But for someone like me, the world isn't that pretty place. It would take nothing but a shoe print in the mud for Vetter to come down on me. I'm sorry I got mad, but I have to stay as far away from the place where a robbery occurred as I can. If you can't understand that, it would be better if I didn't stay here."

Maybe she had misunderstood what it was like to be him because she looked at the world through her lens. She had never been accused of something she hadn't done. She certainly had never been arrested. Just the same, his harsh words had still stung. She thought they were becoming friends again, and she couldn't deny being attracted to him still. She really should learn how to read the room better.

"You're right. I used to believe if I followed all the rules nothing bad would happen to me. That was a foolish belief. I know better now. I'm sorry. I should've known that with your history, even if you followed every single rule to the letter, accusations could still land on your head."

"Thank you for saying that, but hang on a second. What

do you mean you used to believe following the rules would keep bad things from you? Did something happen?"

Her phone rang in the other room. "I have to get that." She hurried away without answering his question. She wasn't prepared to discuss what had happened to her with him. Right now, he didn't look at her with pity or disgust. If he knew the details of her attack, that could change, and she didn't want that. Not from Caleb because he saw her as strong, as the same person she was before.

A picture of Cordy with a high-voltage smile on her weathered face and Alistair the alpaca in his tan-colored beauty lit up the phone screen. Her heart ached to see her grandmother. Her vibrancy filled in all the empty spaces around here that were now dull and lifeless without her.

"Hey, Gram." She grabbed her car keys and put them by the banana bread. It appeared she would be driving over to Mrs. H's after all. As soon as she hung up with Cordy, she'd leave before it got any later.

"Brooklyn, honey, you have to stop calling me Gram. It makes me feel like an old buzzard." Women laughing and clinking glasses drifted through the phone as the noise was somewhere behind Cordy.

"It's what I've called you my whole life." And Cordy, which was what her grandmother preferred, but right now she needed her grandmother to put her arms around her and hold her close until the shakes stopped and she wasn't afraid to go out in the dark. Cordy's love was much like the blankets she knitted with the alpaca fleece—soft and warm.

"And I've been trying to stop you for the past twenty years. If your stubborn mother had listened to me, you and Brad would've called me Sassy or La La instead of Gram."

"Do you want me to start calling you Sassy now?" She kicked off her slippers and shoved her feet into her boots by the door. Cordy was sassy, if nothing else.

"Cordy will do. Besides, your brother will never catch on. Anyhoo, I didn't call to discuss my name, obviously. I called to tell you I've made a decision."

Her spine snapped straight. "What kind of a decision?" With Cordy, a declaration like that could mean anything from her planning to take a six-month cruise to her wanting to plant fig trees to her wanting to paint the house from top to bottom in a buffalo plaid.

"It's very spur of the moment. I hadn't given it a lot of thought before this trip out west, but now that I've been here a few weeks and I've seen this beautiful place I've decided."

"Decided what?"

"I'm going to sell the farm."

CHAPTER FIVE

C aleb wanted to put his fist through the wall. Stopping
at the bar the other night was one of the biggest
mistakes he had made in a long time. Because he had allowed
a sliver of sentiment to seep from his heart, he was now
trapped in Brooklyn's guest room angrier than a cornered
bear. And that piece of shit, Officer Vetter, was looking at him
for a crime he had nothing to do with. Again.

He just wanted to get on his bike and get the hell out of
town. He dug his phone out of his pocket and searched his
contacts. He would leave the bike until it was finished. He
didn't need to stay in a town where no one understood him.
He had actually hoped for a second that Brooklyn would
remember the him before he went to prison. He wanted her
to see the man who had held her in his arms under the
moonlight, the man who had been scared to death to make
love to her.

He had a friend in North Jersey a small town called
Silent Water. His friend was a cook in a little dump of a
restaurant Caleb had worked at for about a year before

coming here. Silent Water was a long drive to Candlewood Falls, but maybe Chase would come for him.

He pulled up Chase's number but didn't hit the dial button. He couldn't ask him to drive all the way down here to rescue him. Caleb ran a hand over his face. What the hell was he thinking? Instead, he searched for a driving service to come and get him. He had no idea where he would go, but anywhere other than here would be fine.

While he downloaded the app, he strained to hear who Brooklyn was talking to. What had she meant about no longer believing following the rules made everything all right? She had run away before answering him.

He had acted like an ass to her. She hadn't deserved that, but he hadn't expected her to ask him to go to Mrs. Holloway's. He had panicked. She had stuck up for him. And what did he do to repay her? He went and dumped all over the gesture. He would apologize again.

The driving service could wait a few minutes. He wanted to talk to her before she left. He eased open the bedroom door. Silence drifted down the hall. Maybe she had already gone next door. He could stick around until he spoke to her. Then he would go.

He would fix something to eat and make extra for her. A decent meal could be part of his apology. He stopped halfway through the threshold into the kitchen. Brooklyn sat at the table staring off into space. Her mouth hung open and her fingers drummed on the table.

"Hey, are you okay?" He circled the table, giving her space.

She blinked a few times. The rims of her eyes were red. "Yeah. Yes." She stood and tugged on the hem of her shirt. "I was just leaving."

"Can you hang on a second? I need to talk to you."

"There's nothing left to say. I understand why you don't

want to come next door. And you were also right about our arrangement having nothing to do with friendship. That ended a long time ago." She tucked the banana bread into her oversized purse and kept her gaze away from him.

"I'm the one who should be sorry. You have been nothing but kind to me, and I didn't return the favor. I'm sorry. It's just when I'm in this town...I don't know. It's like I can't breathe or something." He risked putting his hand on her arm. He kept his touch light so she wouldn't jump. "I shouldn't have spoken to you that way. I know better now. I promise."

"Your response was typical Caleb."

"I never took my anger out on you." He had been an enraged kid, getting into fights whenever it suited him, but he had never raised a hand to a woman and never would. Especially not Brooklyn.

"I don't want to talk about the past. We aren't those people anymore. That was a lifetime ago. If you'll excuse me, I want to get next door before it gets any later. Will you be here when I get back?"

"Do you want me to be?" He held his breath. If she wanted him gone, he would go without an argument, but he didn't really want to leave her. He did want out of the town, but being with Brooklyn reminded him he might still be worth something because she had been the person who had believed he was worth something once.

"I rented you the room, didn't I?" She looked up at him through her lashes and half smiled.

"Aren't you worried I might get angry again?" The tightness in his chest eased some because of her smile.

"You will get angry again. But I don't think you'll hurt me."

"Are you sure that's how you feel?" He needed her to believe that he would never raise a hand to her. He had been in plenty of fights. He had even pulled a knife on a man once, but only because the guy had tried to steal his money. The knife had scratched the guy's side barely leaving a mark, but he had ended up in jail for that one because he couldn't afford the bail. He went to court and the guy never showed so the prosecutor dropped the charges. The guy hadn't even gone to see Doc. But Caleb would never hurt her. Not on purpose.

"Will you put your hands on me?" Her words startled him.

"Not that way. Never you." Vetter had put those thoughts in her head. If only he hadn't come upon SJ Wilde that night in the alley. His life would have been so much different. He would have a place to call home and maybe a woman to love.

"Then that's settled. You'll stay until your bike is fixed." She swung her purse over her shoulder and headed for the door. He almost asked if she still wanted the company, but he kept his mouth shut.

"What had you so upset when I came into the room? You looked like you lost a good friend." He couldn't stop the need to know. He wanted to fix whatever it was if he could.

She hesitated with her hand on the knob. Her shoulders heaved, but she didn't turn to face him. "Nothing that concerns you." She closed the door without another word, leaving him alone with his anger and the ticking of that damn clock in the other room.

"Well, you fucked that up royally," he said to himself.

He went back to his phone and opened the driving service app. She had said she wanted him to stay. The idea of spending some time with her spread heat over his skin. He had wanted to see her and talk to her for years, but he would never have reached out to her. She had married a good man and made a good life for herself. He had been the one to ruin everything. He hadn't the right to disrupt her life. Now he could spend a few days getting to know her again. Maybe even find out what has her tied in knots. He would be risking his freedom because if Vetter could find one shred of evidence to point to him, he was done for.

"You'd be smart to get the hell out of here," he said to the empty room. But that sentimental sliver had become more of a gash after he saw the tears in her eyes. He wanted to help her.

Just like before.

She sat up screaming. The room was dark. Brooklyn's heart pummeled her chest hard enough that her ribs fought to keep it in place. She tried to suck in a breath, but her lungs didn't cooperate.

The bedroom door swung open. The dim light from the hallway spilled in behind the silhouette of a large man. She screamed again. She would fight this time.

The man dropped down on the bed, trying to grab her wrists. "Brooklyn, Brooklyn, it's me. It's Caleb. You're all right." He struggled against her flailing. "Babe, it's me." He grasped her wrists and held them away from his face.

The familiar cadence of his words cleared some of the sleep fog in her brain. She had another nightmare. Her heart still raced, but each breath she took stretched out, filling the bottom of her lungs. She wrapped her arms around his waist and slumped against him, the fight gone out of her. Heat rolled off his bare muscular chest. His skin smelled woodsy and like cedar, comforting. She closed her eyes and trembled.

"Hey." He gathered the blanket around her. "I think you were having a pretty bad nightmare." He eased out of her hold and brushed the hair from her face. "Do you want to talk about it?"

She shook her head because the words had tangled in her throat. She couldn't tell him. He would be revolted like Oliver had been. Oliver had stopped touching her. Even the smallest of gestures made him cringe. She couldn't bear to see that same look on Caleb's face.

"Can I get you something?" His hands cupped her face. He had strong hands that had broken jaws, but against her skin, his touch was soft and gentle.

"No, thank you. I'll be fine. This just happens once in a while." She gripped his hands and held them in her lap. His knuckles were thick and misshapen, but those rugged hands could keep her safe. Inviting him here had been the right thing to do. Endless nights filled with frightening dreams were better shared.

"It's not normal to have the kind of nightmares that wake you up screaming. You yelled so loudly, I thought someone had broken in here this time." He squeezed her hands.

"I'm sorry." Her words scratched her dry throat, giving her the voice of a pack a day smoker. She swallowed and tried again. "I didn't mean to wake you." She had had a few nightmares before Cordy went on vacation. The poor woman had come in here yielding a baseball bat in her nightgown. Before that, it had been months since her last one. She had actually thought she was over them.

"No problem. If you're okay, I'm going to try and get a few more hours of sleep. Those alpacas get up early." He stood and the mattress shifted with the loss of his weight.

"Caleb?"

"Yeah?"

"Could you stay until I fall asleep?" She didn't want to be alone. She doubted sleep would return anymore. For the rest of the night every time she closed her eyes, she would see *him*. The nightmares stole what little peace she had managed to garnish. The therapist had said they would go away in time, but they hadn't. She never knew what would bring one on so she never knew how to prepare for them.

Earlier, at Mrs. Holloway's she had listened to the woman's recanting of her own attack. The story must've triggered her nightmares. She had wondered why Mrs. H would even stay in her house, but that feisty old lady said she wouldn't be thrown from her house by a hoodlum.

He ran a hand over his face and scratched at the growth on his chin. "Sure."

He dropped into the rocking chair in the corner. The old dry wood creaked in response. She settled back down and brought the blankets up to her chin. The remnants of the bad dream still made her blood run cold. Some nights she worried she'd never be warm again.

"This might be a lot to ask, but do you think you could lie down beside me?" She wanted his heat to keep her warm, nothing more.

"I don't think that's a good idea. I'll just sit here until you fall asleep."

"You're right. I don't know what I was thinking. Thank you for staying." She turned her back to him. She would be fine with Caleb in the chair across from her. She didn't need him in the bed beside her. That would make their situation more awkward than it already was.

She was used to juggling her emotional needs by herself, anyway, from a mother who ran faster than a greyhound away from her children, to an ex-husband who wouldn't know an emotion if it cried and screamed in his face.

But she wanted Caleb pressed against her, to have the strength of his muscles to lean into. In his arms, she was protected. That protection gave way to something else. Something bolder. He had lit a heat in her, hotter than she had felt in years.

When she and Oliver were first married, she hadn't

noticed his inability to express any emotion. She was busy with nursing school and working long hours in the emergency room then she had moved to the maternity floor. Babies came at all hours, and she wanted to be around for the deliveries which meant working the graveyard shift when Oliver worked days.

But after her attack, when all she wanted was him to hold her and tell her everything would be okay, he was incapable of seeing her break down. The attack and Oliver had doused any desire to be intimate. Instead of loving her, Oliver had left her.

The rocking chair scraped against the floor with a creak and a groan. Caleb lifted the covers and slid onto the bed, gathering her against his solid chest. She relaxed in the tenderness of his embrace.

"What made you change your mind?" She tried not to think about the way the muscles of his front-body pressed against her thin t-shirt, or the way his strong leg looped over hers. His body was fit and gave refuge. She craved some of that security the way a junkie craved his next fix.

"If a dream could have you screaming like that, something must be bothering you pretty bad. And if you're asking me to hold you, then maybe you trust me a little."

This embrace might mean as much to him as it did for her, but for different reasons. In the moment, she did not care about his history of fighting, and she did not believe he was a killer. This man holding her in her time of need was her Caleb, the young man she used to know.

"I trust you."

"Brooks?" he whispered against her hair, the long-forgotten nickname he had given her. She wouldn't ask him to stop. She had always liked the sound of it rolling off his lips.

"Yes?"

"What had you upset earlier? Before you went next door." He kept his voice low and stroked her arm with his fingers, waking up every nerve ending in her body.

"Cordy is selling the farm." This subject was easier to talk about than the nightmares, and he might ask again about what had her screaming.

"What? When?"

"Apparently, her vacation inspired her. She made the decision just this morning. She called Brad first to tell him so he could make an offer." The tears tried to return again, but she was tired of crying. Cordy's declaration had ripped her heart in half. She had every right to sell her farm, but to give Brad the chance to buy it over her was as if she didn't exist. She thought Cordy knew what the farm meant to her.

"What did he say?"

"He's going to buy it as soon as he can. He wants the land for more trees. He's going to get rid of the alpacas." She fought to keep the tears hidden, but one leaked out.

"Cordy is okay with him selling the alpacas?" His fingers made longer strokes up and down her arm.

Her skin sizzled with his touch. A response she hadn't expected. She had wanted only some comfort, and he had held her in his arms a long time ago. Asking him to hold her again was like muscle memory.

She almost asked him to touch her in other places. Almost. She needed more time to gather her nerve. She hadn't thought about the consequences before she had asked him to climb into bed with her. He had been familiar, and the nightmare had made her afraid. Now, their bodies touching reminded her of other stolen nights just like this. Parts of her remembered too well.

"It seems that way. She's going to make sure they all stay together and get a good home."

"And what about you?" he said.

"What about me?" She wasn't sure what he was asking exactly. Her mind was focused on his hands moving from her arm to her hip.

"Isn't this your home too?"

"I thought it was, but I was wrong. Now I don't have a home." She couldn't believe Cordy wouldn't consider her feelings or thoughts about selling the alpaca farm. She had purposely come home to her to heal and find her way again. She hadn't finished that task yet. She had more to do, and if she had to find another place to live, to start again when she had barely gotten her sea legs under her, she would not make it. She needed to stay here.

"Why can't you offer to buy the farm too?"

She turned in his arms to look at him. "I hadn't thought about it until she called. I figured she would live here for the rest of her life and that I had time to make decisions about my future. Now that she's yanked the farm out from under me, I see what I want even if I can't knit."

She had stared at that basket of yarn Cordy had dangled in front of her for months now. Cordy had been on her to knit since she arrived back in the spring, but she had protested. At first, she had blamed her lack of desire on being too tired, but once she had spent some time on the farm and let the sun soak into her skin and the alpacas love her, she had more energy than she had had in a long time. The farm had agreed with her.

"I watched you with the alpacas tonight. You know how to take care of them, and what you don't know Cordy will show you. I can help you with some of the other stuff around here. Your fence needs fixing, and the roof of the barn is leaking." He pushed up on his elbow, bringing his gaze closer to hers. His woodsy scent surrounded her again. He was right about the things needing attention. Cordy had allowed some of the wear to show around here, even in the house. The upkeep was part of the reason she wanted to sell. She was ready to have more fun in her golden years.

Caleb was also right about her and the alpacas. She had fallen in love with all five of them. She enjoyed seeing the boys and girls every morning when she brought them breakfast. Each one greeted her in their own special way. They nuzzled her when she ran her fingers over their soft fleece. They were very self-sufficient for the most part. She had even gone with Cordy a few times to the orchard with them when the orchard had an event. And this week was her first lunch with the alpacas without Cordy.

"You would stick around and help me?"

"I could stay for a little while. I'm in between jobs at the moment. And I'm pretty good with my hands." He wiggled his fingers.

Heat flushed her face and she was grateful for the shadows of the room because he wasn't coming onto her. Her body's response to his statement was simply old habits. Caleb and she would never be together that way again, even if the idea was more than appealing.

"What about Officer Vetter?"

He flopped back on the bed and looked up at the ceiling. "I almost forgot about him. What if I stay until my bike gets fixed, and then we see? Maybe the real suspect will be caught and Vetter can get off my ass."

"I have a lot to consider. Like how would I even come up with the money to outbid Brad?" And what she would do when Caleb left town. If he were to help her fix things up around here and left before they were finished, she would have to hire someone else. But that wasn't her real problem because an ad posted in the coffeehouse or in Vivian's hair salon would fix that right up. She was more concerned about getting used to having Caleb near her and then having to let him go.

She slid out of bed.

"Where are you going?"

"I don't know if I can sleep. My brain is racing. You can stay there though. I'll come back a little later."

He threw his legs over the side and stood inches from her. He brushed her hair away from her face. "Brooklyn Wilde, thank you for the offer, but the next time I'm asleep in your bed, I want it to be for different reasons."

He placed a soft kiss on her cheek and left her alone. With more things on her mind besides buying the farm.

CHAPTER SIX

C aleb made his way past the "Pick Your Own" apple trees where mothers with their children, school tours, and couples pulled the best and brightest apples off the branches. Wilde Orchards provided rows and rows of varying tree varieties, allowing customers to gather several different types of apples into brown bags. The sweet smell of ripe fruit was thick enough to spread. The sun beat down on the back of his neck, and the humidity hung in the air like a wet blanket. Summer kept a stubborn hold on fall's weather.

He needed to find Brad. The woman inside the store where they sold apples, donuts, and cider had said he was out by the cold storage barn, supervising the shipment for wholesalers.

Caleb hadn't told Brad he was coming over here, because he knew Brad would brush him off or tell him to stay away. But after being torn from sleep by Brooklyn's piercing screams, he wanted to find out what Brad knew about Brooklyn's nightmares. Even though he promised to stick around and help her, he wasn't sure he could go through with it. The minute his bike was ready, he might need to be on it and the highway out of here. He couldn't allow Officer Vetter to throw him in jail. If that happened, he would never get out again. He'd rather be dead than incarcerated for something he didn't do—twice.

Holding Brooklyn last night had reminded him how lonely he was, roaming from town to town never putting down roots. He never held a woman all night anymore. He didn't see the point in getting attached to anyone if he would just move on when the town borders began to confine him. But her scent of flowers and soap eased the tension in his chest. She had pressed her soft curves against his hard lines, trusting him to keep her safe. He had wanted to hold her all night just like that. She fit him. He had forgotten about that.

When she had slid out of bed, he was disappointed and relieved at the same time. If he had stayed with her backside against his groin much longer, he might've tried to kiss her. Even now he could still feel the pressure of her body against his. Brooklyn tempted something in him better left alone. He would only bring her trouble.

The cold storage barn stretched into the bright sky with its cedar planks and pointed roof. Some guy operated a forklift, picking up large pallets of apples and bringing them to a truck idling off to the side.

"Raf, bring her forward a little more." Brad waved the forklift driver closer to the pallet. The muscles on his arms flexed with the movement. Brad had been in about as many fights as he had as a kid, but the biggest difference was Brad belonged to the Wilde family, and no one came down too hard on Brad. Some were even willing to look the other way.

The Wildes were well-respected and a permanent fixture in this town. They had been around almost as long as the town itself. Caleb had just been a caretaker's son. His father couldn't hold his liquor and couldn't keep his hands to himself. He had taken things that didn't belong to him. Caleb's father was not a pillar of the community.

The man named Raf gave him a thumbs-up and scooped up the pallet. Another guy, tall and lanky with red hair and a face full of freckles hurried by carrying a clipboard. If memory served him, that was Sam Wilde. The son of the man he had been accused of killing. Caleb froze. Coming to the orchard had been a stupid mistake. He had made a few too many of those, lately and it was going to cost him. Anyone from the Wilde family, and there were plenty, could pounce on him.

"Hi. Can I help you with something?" the red-haired guy said, stopping only inches away. Up close there was no mistaking this was Sam Wilde. He had the same bright-blue eyes as his father had. Caleb remembered those eyes, vacant and lifeless, staring up at him.

"Sam, I'm looking for Brad." He braced himself for the tirade of assaults that would come at him. Sam Wilde would want to tear him limb from limb, believing he was the man who caused his father's death.

"Have we met?" Sam narrowed his eyes. "Wait a second. You're Caleb Ransom."

He didn't want to fight this man, but he didn't think he could stand there and take a beating either. He had been wronged in the whole episode too. He hadn't killed SJ, and the police never found out who did. His release on a technicality made no difference to many people in this town. Why should it make a difference to Sam Wilde?

"That's right. I am." He held Sam's gaze. He had nothing to be ashamed of and every right to be in Candlewood Falls.

"I heard you were in town. Did you lose your way around the orchard? We don't allow customers back here. It isn't safe." Sam held the clipboard loosely at his side. His shoulders were relaxed and his stance unguarded.

Why wasn't this guy yelling at him or demanding he leave the orchard? He was certain the son who had lost his father to murder would hate the person accused, even if that person was wrongly so.

"I...I...I'm sorry about your father, but I didn't kill him." He had to say it, had to make it as clear as he could. He would never take a life. Ever. If only he had come upon SJ minutes sooner, he might have lived and been able to say who had beat him hard enough to kill him.

"I don't blame you for my father's death." Sam stuck out his hand.

He stared at it, unsure what to do. He hadn't expected this reaction from Sam. He tried to get his mind around it. Plenty of people in town still hated him for allegedly killing a beloved Wilde, and yet here was Sam showing him a random act of kindness. If only Brooklyn's father and brother felt the same way as her cousin.

"What the hell are you doing here?" An angry voice vibrated over the loud forklift.

He turned away from Sam and his extended hand. Brad marched over, kicking up rocks and dirt. He stopped and fisted his hands on his hips. His top lip curled up and fury slashed across his eyes.

"He's looking for you," Sam said.

"Yeah, well I'm standing right here, and I don't want to see you on my property." Brad pointed a finger in his face.

"If you two will excuse me, I have some chutney to check on," Sam said and walked away. Caleb was glad to see him go. His business was with Brad. He didn't want anyone else involved, least of all Sam because he wasn't sure he could trust Sam's reaction to him.

"I only need a minute." And it would be only a minute because he didn't want to be here one second longer than he had to.

Brad wiped his brow with his work glove. "I don't have time for you. Some of us work, you know."

He knew how hard Brad worked on this orchard. He had worked here a couple of summers when they were teenagers. Brad had been trying to run the whole place back then. Brad had worked in the orchard, picking the apples that would be sold to wholesalers and retailers side by side with all the employees. Brad had grafted trees and ran the machines. Caleb had checked, over the years, on the orchard. Brad was now the vice president of operations. He wasn't surprised.

"It's about Brooklyn." Maybe that would be the one thing that would make Brad listen.

"What about her?" Brad narrowed his eyes.

"I think something is bothering her." He wanted to tread lightly with what he offered because Brooklyn didn't know he was here and probably wouldn't want him talking to her brother, but if he had to leave town in a hurry, he wanted Brad to know something was wrong. Brad might be able to convince her to talk to someone. He just didn't want to leave without knowing at least one person was looking out for her. Someone besides Cordy who was also ready to leave her in the dust.

"Yeah? What's bothering her now? Her dumbass ex-husband calling? Or is she pissed because I'm getting the farm and she isn't? Because if that's the problem, I can't help her. I'm buying Cordy's farm."

"How is it that you two are related? She's your sister, man. I come here to tell you she might need help and you start shooting your mouth off. I know you hate me, but what's your problem with her?"

"I can't help my sister because she won't let me. She doesn't let anyone help her. I told her to stay away from you. She didn't listen to me on that one."

"I think telling her what to do and offering assistance are

very different things. She can make her own decisions about her friends. Something big is bothering her. I'm concerned."

The guy driving the forklift honked the horn and held up his hands in question.

"Hang on a second, Raf," Brad said then turned back to him. "Nothing for you to be concerned about. The Wildes look out for each other. We're a big family. If she needs something, she has plenty of people all around here ready to help her. So, whatever you think you know, forget about it. You don't know anything about her anymore."

Brad was right about that much, but he was wrong about Brooklyn having people to lean on. She didn't feel that way at the moment, and there was a reason for that. It might be because her brother was a self-centered ass who thought he knew it all. Not much different than their father who also had an opinion about everything she did. And everyone in town knew Huck Wilde ran a local group for men who felt superior to every race and gender. That self-righteous streak ran deep in this family. Somehow, Brooklyn had missed it.

"I'm sorry to have bothered you." It had been a waste of time to come here. He turned to leave.

"Let me give you a piece of advice."

He stopped and met Brad's gaze. Brad didn't wait for him to say he wanted to hear the unsolicited advice.

"You should get that bike of yours and get out of town before something bad happens to you. That wipeout you had wasn't any accident. If you're not careful, you could be hurt a lot worse next time."

"Are you threatening me?" A cold shiver ran over his skin even standing in the sun's heat. He took two steps forward, closing the space between them.

"Just a concerned member of society." Brad tipped two fingers and went back to the forklift.

His insides burned. Brad knew something about the accident. He must know who had been in that car that had cut him off. But he hadn't seen Brad at the bar that night. What was Brad a part of? Could that same person have broken into Mrs. Holloway's house, hoping to pin it on him? He really did need to get out of town. And fast.

Brooklyn climbed out of her car in a cold sweat. The road leading to her father's cabin wasn't much more than dirt and every time it rained the road seemed to wash away with it. Her teeth rattled along every drop and curve. She had white-knuckled it until his cabin came into view.

The space, though, was beautiful with the tall oak trees and whispering pines surrounding the small log cabin. Her father had built a porch where he could sit and watch the sun set. Out back was a matching porch to watch sunrises. He had two other buildings on the property. One was the outhouse and the other the storage shed filled with supplies if the end of the world ever did happen.

She took a cleansing breath. The rolling hills accented the sky. This time of year the burst of fall colors set those rolling hills on fire. She understood why her father loved this place so much. She just wished he had running water.

She also wished he was alone for this visit. Her uncle Huck's old model pickup was there. A visit from her uncle never meant anything good. He always tried to cause trouble between the five brothers. He was so different from the rest of the family, and she didn't understand why. Her grandparents were sweet people and well respected in the community. At least Grandpa Skip still was. Grandma Evelyn had passed away years ago. How had they raised a man like Huck?

She didn't bother to knock. This had been her home once. She belonged there more than Huck did. Inside, the two men sat at the small table built for three in the corner of the kitchen area which wasn't much more than an icebox and a toaster. Her father ran electricity off a propane generator. A bottle of whiskey and two glasses were on the table.

"Hey, Brooklyn." Her father pushed his large frame out of the spindle back chair. It creaked with relief. Even at his fifty-nine years, her dad was in good shape. Brad had taken after him. They had the same body type and strong features. She had favored her mother's side more.

Dad's face broke out in a wide smile which deepened the lines around his blue eyes. He held out his arms and she went into them, soaking up his love for her. He smelled like wood chips and fresh air.

"Hi, Daddy. Hello, Uncle Huck." She nodded in the man's direction.

"Afternoon, Brooklyn. I hear you have a visitor down at Cordy's place." He stood his full height, the same as her father's, and crossed his arms over his chest.

"I do." She wasn't going to give him more than that. Caleb was none of his business.

"You don't want a man like that under your roof. For one it doesn't look good. You're a married woman. And for another, he's a murderer. Have you forgotten he killed our brother SJ?"

As if anyone in their family was going to forget how SJ had died. "I am no longer married so I am free to publicly have a male guest, but thank you for being concerned about my virtue. And the other thing you should try to get straight is Caleb didn't kill SJ. The police never found out who did." The police were never going to figure it out either. Too many years had gone by and any trail would be ice cold by now. After Caleb went away, no one had a reason to keep looking.

"That's not how I see it." Huck smirked and drained the last of his drink.

"Huck, that's enough. Weren't you just leaving?" Her dad's voice held a warning tone.

"Silas, I meant what I said. Control your family." Huck pointed a finger at her dad and walked out without another word.

"What did he mean about controlling your family?"

"Don't worry about him. Huck is always a lot of hot air. Come and sit." Dad removed the glass Huck had used.

"Dad, he's a lot more than hot air. He leads a group of men ready to do whatever he says. And he doesn't hide the fact he doesn't like people different than he is."

"That club of old men aren't going to do anything to or for anyone. They just sit around that hall smoking and drinking and complaining."

"I don't know. I don't think it's that simple. Did he say something about me?" Her uncle always had it in for Caleb even before SJ died. Huck didn't like the idea she had been hanging around with him when they were kids. He had said spending time with the likes of Caleb Ransom made the family look bad.

"He didn't say anything about you. Forget Huck. What brings you by?" His smile spread wide with the change of subject.

She wasn't entirely sure she believed her father, but he wasn't going to say anything more about Huck. When he was done with a conversation, he was done. "I wanted to ask you something."

"Ask away."

"Can I borrow some money?"

"Sure. How much do you need? I have a couple hundred on me. If you need more, I have to go to the safe." He reached into the back pocket of his jeans and pulled out his worn leather wallet. She had given him that wallet as a

Christmas present when she was still in high school. She shook her head. New and fancy were not his things.

She placed a hand over his. "Not that kind of money. Real money. I want to buy Cordy's farm."

"Cordy's selling her farm? Since when?"

"Since about five minutes ago. Cordy decided on vacation she's tired of winters in New Jersey. She wants to move to Arizona." She still couldn't believe it was true, but an impulsive decision was just like Cordy. She led with her heart and almost never her head. Things always seemed to work out for her that way. Brooklyn was a little more than envious of Cordy's free spirit.

"She never did think things through." Her father echoed her thoughts.

"That's exactly why she ended up with an alpaca farm." Cordy had visited a farm decades ago. Met a few alpacas and fell in love with them. Before anyone knew it, she and Grandpa Levon had purchased the land for the farm.

"Cheeks, I would love to give you money, but that much money is tied up."

"In what? Mason jars buried in the back?"

"Some." He winked. "You'll need a lot more than I have access to. I'd have to borrow against my share of the orchard. I don't want to do that because I want you and Brad to decide what to do with the land after I die. If it's tied up with the bank, then the bank has control."

"Dad, you're fifty-nine. You're not dying anytime soon." She couldn't stand the idea of him being gone. When her mother left her father all those years ago, she had barely returned for her children, leaving them practically motherless. Her father had stepped in and done everything he could to be both mother and father to his children. He loved them fiercely. Without his love to keep her grounded, she would fly away.

"Maybe not. I hope not. I'd like to see some grandbabies before I go. I'm really sorry. You know I would do anything for you, but I can't owe the bank. All it would take is one misstep from that industry or another real estate bust, and I'd lose everything. Maybe you could work out a deal with Cordy? Make payments or something."

"She's already asked Brad if he wanted to buy it, and he said yes." She had suspected he would say no. He didn't trust banks or corporations or the government. He barely trusted his brothers and his nephew Sam with the orchard. The one thing that kept him on solid ground with the family business was that Brad was the vice president of operations. Dad trusted Brad.

"Then why are you looking to buy it too?" Dad went to the icebox and pulled out lettuce, tomatoes, and goat cheese. "Do you want lunch? I was going to make a sandwich once Huck got out of here."

"No, thanks. I'm not hungry. I want the farm because it's the only place I feel at home these days. Because I love the alpacas. Because I thought I could stay there for as long as I wanted." The farm had been her other home. When she was growing up, she was either on the orchard or at Cordy's. Cordy was her second chance mother.

"You mean like putting down roots?" He moved around the kitchen, almost hitting his head where the ceiling sloped down.

"I guess. Candlewood Falls was my childhood home. I didn't realize I wanted it to be my forever home until it couldn't be." The moment Cordy had said Brad wanted the land she knew she did too. It could be because she and Brad had always competed for attention in their family. Probably because they were twins and starved for a mother's love, but when she had time to sit with the idea of taking over the alpaca farm, a warm feeling settled in her bones. She belonged there with those silly animals. They made her smile with their personalities and their love.

"Candlewood Falls has a way of calling you home. If you can't live at the farm, why not buy another place?"

"I don't want any other place."

"That stubborn streak is going to get you into trouble." He spread mayonnaise on a roll and added the cheese, lettuce, and tomatoes.

"I got that from you."

"And look what's happened to me." He waved his hand. "I was hell-bent on living alone. I got what I wanted."

"But you love your life." She had never considered for a second her father might be lonely. He never said, but she never asked either. He just went about his business and being her rock when she needed one.

"I do, and I don't think there's a woman out there willing to put up with me." He brought the sandwich and a bottled water to the table. "You should love your life as much. If you want the farm, find a way to get the money. I'll have a talk with Brad."

"He's going to get mad and say you're taking my side like you always do."

"I don't take sides. You've had a setback and could use a leg up. He's doing just fine at the orchard the way it is. They don't need to expand right now."

"Thanks, Dad. So, are you going to tell me what Uncle Huck wanted?"

Her father held his food halfway to his mouth. "He's gunning for Caleb. He doesn't want him around, especially around you."

She gripped the side of the table and took a deep breath. She would not tell Caleb to go just because her narrow-minded uncle thought she should. Her father was right about her stubborn side. "What did you say?"

"I told him my children were grown and none of his business. I also told him we don't really know who killed SJ."

"You did? Since when did you start believing that?"

"The second my brother showed up at my door. When a man protests too hard, he's hiding something. I know Huck didn't hurt SJ, but I have a feeling he knows who did."

CHAPTER SEVEN

The tourists came for miles to Candlewood Falls this time of year. They wanted to walk up and down Main Street, snaking in and out of the shops. Caleb didn't care about the bookstore or the place where the lady read your future on some set of cards. He didn't want to sit in one of the restaurants that faced the water and enjoy a drink. All he wanted was his bike fixed. The small confines of Candlewood Falls closed in around his neck. He had overstayed his welcome. Too many people didn't want him here. He didn't need to be told twice.

He crossed the street to Hafrey's Garage, hoping to get an update from Jameson. A lanky teenager with a greasy Hafrey's Garage cap pulled low on his head pumped gas into a shiny Lexus while the female driver scrolled through her phone.

"Hey, is Jameson around?" he said.

The teen pulled the gas nozzle out of the car and returned it to the pump. He swiped the credit card and attempted to hand it back to the woman. "Nope. He's taking a break. Is there something I can help you with?" He tapped on the

Lexus's window. The woman inside jumped and put her phone down. She snagged her credit card and hurried out into traffic.

"I was wondering when my motorcycle would be done."

"Tourists. They act like they're doing me the favor. I wish they could pump their own gas."

"Then you wouldn't have a job."

"I'd get another one." The idealism of youth could carry the weight of the universe, but was as fragile as a soap bubble. He wished he still felt that way. But he no longer believed he was entitled to the future he wanted. Someone else always held the strings and decided whether or not you could work there, live there, or even love there.

"So, any idea when my bike will be done?"

"No idea. Sorry. Jameson does all the mechanic stuff. I just fill gas tanks." Another car pulled up to the pump. The young man heaved a heavy sigh and went to the driver's window.

"Do you know when he'll be back?"

"He went across the street to the Green Bean. You could probably catch him there." He returned to the task of putting gas into the tanks of others.

"Thanks."

The Green Bean was a new edition since he left. He went inside and was met with the strong smell of freshly brewed coffee. He inhaled. The place was artsy the way he would expect a local coffeehouse to be. He was used to grabbing coffee at any convenience store in his path. He wasn't particular, but the full-flavored smell he was sure would cling to his clothes after he left made him want to get in line.

Instead, he searched for Jameson and found him at a table in the corner with his head buried in his phone, ignoring the tall cup of coffee and the half-eaten muffin.

Whatever Jameson was looking at had him consumed. Caleb weaved around other tables until he got to the mechanic.

"Jameson."

His head snapped up. It took a second for Jameson's eyes to fill with recognition. "Hey, Caleb. Have a seat." He moved the coffee and the muffin to the side.

"Thanks." He slid in the seat opposite. "Sorry to bother you on your break, but your employee said you'd be here."

"That's Dominick. Good kid. What's up?"

"Any word on my bike?"

"Nothing yet. I'm still waiting on some of the parts. The manufacturer was having some shipping issues. You're probably in a hurry to get back on the road."

He could say that again. "What makes you say that?"

Jameson arched a brow. "I would be if I were you. I've heard the whispers. Mrs. Holloway gets burglarized the night you show up. And then you move in with Brooklyn Wilde."

"I didn't move in." And he wouldn't be staying too long either. His leaving was best for everyone.

"That's not what it looks like to the nosey people of this town."

He didn't care what it looked like, but he should. For her. His presence was causing her problems, and she didn't need that. "How soon can you have that bike ready? I need to hit the road."

"I'll see what I can do to rush the parts. But once I get them, I still need a few days."

"Thanks, Jameson." He stuck out his hand.

Jameson waved him away. "No need to thank me. You need someone in your corner. I know what the people of this town can be like. The old buzzard Sofia Dressler got her hooks in me once and weaved an entire untrue story. Broke up my marriage because my ex-wife was too dumb to realize not a word of it was true. I guess that's not on Sofia. Just watch your back in the meantime."

"Will do." He pushed out of the chair. He'd get a cup of coffee to go and one for Brooklyn. Screw the people of this town and their damn gossip mill. He wouldn't let them tell him what to do or who to do it with. He wasn't a coward who ran away from a fight, and Brooklyn wanted him around. She had even wanted him to hold her when she was scared. What would Sofia Dressler say about that?

He took the spot at the end of the line. A hand gripped his shoulder and whipped him around. He raised his hands to throw a punch but stopped. Brad Wilde stared at him with rage-filled eyes.

"What do you think you're doing getting mixed up in my family's business?" A vein pulsed on the side of his neck.

"Did you follow me here?" He had left the orchard on foot and walked back into town, looking for Jameson.

"No, you dumbass. I got a visitor after you left this morning. You're sticking your nose where it doesn't belong, and I don't appreciate it."

Heads turned. The constant buzzing of conversation dwindled to silence.

"Not sure what you're talking about, but I don't think you want to have that discussion here." He didn't know who would've come to the orchard after he left. If it had been Brooklyn, why wouldn't she have come to him first?

Brad looked around as if he just realized where he was standing. Brad wouldn't want to give anyone a big piece of gossip to chew on, and they would. If he knew anything about Brad, he knew Brad was as private as he was. In some other life, they might have been friends.

Good thing Weezer River wasn't here. She lived for the gossip, but unlike Sofia Dressler, Weezer never made up stories.

On cue, Brad turned on his heel and swaggered out the door. So much for the cup of coffee he wanted. Without much choice, he followed Brad out. The door swung closed on the wind of loud whispers.

They stood in the walkway between the coffee shop and the empty building and out of the way of anyone walking by.

"Why did you tell my sister to make an offer on Cordy's farm?"

"Still not sure what you're talking about." He had put the thought in Brooklyn's head while they lay in bed together last night. He didn't see any good reason why Brooklyn should be pushed out of her home and be replaced by apple trees. The orchard had plenty of trees and business. Maybe Brad should be more concerned about his sister than his pocket.

"She never wanted the farm before you showed up. She hasn't even lived in town in the past ten years. She knows nothing about alpacas, and now she wants to become an alpaca farmer."

"She has the right to make Cordy an offer."

"You should mind your own business. You don't know my sister anymore. You don't know what she went through last year. She's fragile and lost. She thinks she wants the farm, but she doesn't. She'll be out of town the second something gets hard. That's what she does. She never sticks around for the difficult stuff." Brad shook his head. "But she always loved the strays. Stay out of my life or the next time I'll take you to the town limits myself." He marched away, not waiting for a response.

Caleb ran both hands over his face and scratched at his jaw. Stopping at the bar for a couple of drinks the other night had turned into a whole web of problems. If he had had somewhere to go or someone waiting for him, he would've driven straight out of town after the cemetery. Instead, he inserted himself smack in the middle of Brooklyn and her family. Or better yet, whoever had caused his accident had aided in shoving him between Brooklyn's problems and her family's.

He hadn't bothered anyone the other night at Murphy's. Hadn't even spoken to anyone. He hadn't thought one extra hour in town, so late at night, could make any difference.

"Ransom, hold up." Officer Vetter held the side of his gun belt and hurried down the walkway from the parking lot. His aviator glasses hid his eyes, but the snarl across his lips didn't line up with happy to see him.

"I'm late for an appointment." He had no appointment but wished he did. He'd even be happy going to the proctologist at this point.

"Too bad. You can be late. I've been looking all over town for you."

"Really? What for? You inviting me to your bachelor party?"

"Stifle it. I have security footage from the bar showing the time you left. Based on the time of Mrs. Holloway's break-in that lines you up with being in the right place at the right time. You've got the bruises to prove you used violence that night. Let me see your hands."

His hands had been scratched up from the fall because he wasn't wearing gloves, especially the knuckles on his right hand. He reluctantly showed Vetter.

"You got those beating up an innocent old lady."

He kept his hands at his sides because one wrong move could have this cop throwing him to the ground and cuffing him. "I fell off my bike. Have you ever fallen on a motorcycle? The rider usually makes out the worst."

"Mrs. Holloway is sitting with a sketch artist as we speak. She's going to give them a description of you. Then I'm coming for you. You made a mistake stepping foot back in my town."

That much Vetter had right. "You don't have anything other than circumstantial evidence. And you're forgetting I have an alibi." Brooklyn had lied for him. He hadn't knocked on her door until after the robbery. If Mrs. Holloway even hinted, he was her assailant he was done for.

"I'll punch holes in that alibi. Don't you worry about that. This time when you go to prison, you'll never get out."

Brooklyn paced the living room while the phone rang. She pressed her cell against her ear until it hurt. She didn't know who else to ask, but she wanted a chance to buy the farm. She peeked out the window. One of the alpacas, Chewpaca, the black one, had lain on his back in the sun, enjoying the afternoon. She shook her head. She wished she could be so carefree. She could learn a few things from the alpacas.

"Hello? Brooklyn? What's going on?" Her ex-husband's familiar voice came across the line.

"Hi, Oliver. How are you?"

"I'm right in the middle of a big deal. I have a lot going on. Can I call you later?" That familiar voice was always coated in impatience and exasperation toward her as if she knew exactly what he was doing and had interrupted him on purpose. He always had the option of not answering, if he were busy, but instead he answered and then tried to make her feel like a burden.

"It's kind of important." She needed to ask now before she lost her nerve.

He let out a long breath. "Okay. Five minutes."

"I want to buy my grandmother's farm."

"With those dirty animals?"

The alpacas weren't dirty. In fact, they were quite clean, but she didn't bother to correct him. He had never liked the farm or the orchard. He wasn't a man who willingly stuck his hands in dirt unless he could save money doing it. He certainly wouldn't get dirty saving her.

"I love the alpacas. They're sweet and funny. They each have a personality, and their fleece is valuable. I've decided to stay on in Candlewood Falls, and I want to buy the farm."

"So, buy the farm. What are you telling me for?"

She had turned down alimony in the divorce. She didn't want his money, especially since she had a job at one time. But she had been unable to work since her attack. Every time she saw a female patient broken and battered, scared out of her mind because she had been accosted, she fell to pieces. She couldn't do her job that way.

All she had asked for was the money from the sale of the house and half their savings. He kept the rest because truthfully, it was more his than hers. He earned three times what she did. The big house and the fancy cars existed in their lives because Oliver made the money.

"I was wondering if you would consider loaning me the down payment." She held her breath. She could find a way to make the mortgage payments. The store where Cordy sold goods made from the alpacas' fleece brought in money. She could expand that to offer other items like local honey and beeswax candles, or add to the places Cordy brought the alpacas for appearances. The worst-case scenario would be her trying to find a part-time nursing position. Maybe Doc needed help.

"You want me to loan you money?" Oliver's strained voice echoed in her head.

It's what she just said, wasn't it? "Yes. I don't have that much money. I won't get the loan to buy the farm without it. I'll pay you back."

"You're going to borrow money from me and the bank?"

Was she speaking in a foreign language? "I can't borrow the full amount. The bank won't allow it." She ran her fingers over the scar on her neck, recalling each bump before she touched it. "I don't have anyone else to ask, Oliver."

"Can't your brother loan you the money? He's always bragging how well the orchard is doing."

"Brad wants to buy the farm too. I have to be able to outbid him."

"You're going into a bidding war over an alpaca farm? What for? Don't you want to go back to nursing? Hang on a second." He said something to someone in the background. "I'm back. Are you considering giving up your stable career as a nurse?"

"I love the animals."

"You will always have a job if you're a nurse, Brooklyn. You should be more practical about this."

"I'm tired of being practical, Oliver. I need a change. I think if I sit down with Brad and explain why I need to live here, he'll back off. He's not coldhearted." She hoped he would back off and not see her wanting the farm as a way to compete with him, but that was a strong possibility. He could decide he had to have the farm too and not budge. His position at the orchard would give him the advantage for a bigger loan. The bank manager practically fell over herself every time Brad walked in. She would open the vault and throw money at him if she thought helping Brad would get her a date.

"You running a farm doesn't seem like a wise investment on my part," Oliver said.

"Can't you do it for old times' sake?" He must've loved her once.

"If you were still my wife, then maybe. But you didn't

want to be my wife any longer." The familiar and tired anger returned to his voice.

"You didn't want to be a husband, or at least not a husband to a woman who had been attacked." She never said the word. Couldn't say the word. If he had been there for her when she needed him most, she would still be married to him. Except he would stay late at work with excuses and come home long after she went to bed. When she reached for him, he shrank away. At first, she thought she was imagining it.

Then one night, about six months after her attack, she had run a bath and shaved her legs. She put on lavender perfume and styled her hair. She had purchased a black night-gown from an online store and let the silky garment slip over her skin. She glanced in the mirror, and for a second she felt sexy again. She had found him sitting up in bed with only his pajama pants on. His belly had softened over the years, but she liked it. He was reading something on his tablet and didn't look up when she approached.

She ran a finger up his arm. A smile tugged at the corner of his lip. A warmth of confidence ran over her. He looked up and took her in, standing there in the fancy nightgown with a dash of lip gloss on her lips. If there had been a smile on his face, it fell off. The light went out of his eyes. He had pushed her hand away and jumped out of bed. He didn't want her to touch him. She packed her bags that night and drove straight to Cordy.

"Brooklyn, I don't want to have this fight again." Oliver's voice startled her back to the present. "I know you went through something horrible. I'm sorry about that, but it affected me too. I know you wanted me to be made of stone or something, but I'm not. What happened to you happened to both of us."

"Not in the same way. I was the real victim. All you had

to do was love me anyway. Look, I didn't call for a shoulder to lean on. Will you lend me the money or not?" He was an egotistical self-absorbed jerk, which she would reserve saying because she did want his money.

"What do I get in return?"

She let out a long breath. He always looked for an angle to benefit himself. He did nothing without putting a price tag to it. "Interest?"

"How about I get to come out to the farm and see where my money is going?"

That was the last thing she wanted. She needed him to stay away from the place that brought her peace. His presence would sully all that she worked for here. He would stick his nose down at the alpacas and the hay barn. The house was old and worn too. He was used to the best luxuries. He would judge her.

"Why would you want to do that?" She forced her voice to stay calm.

"No one invests in a business without looking it over. Besides, it would be nice to see you."

He was up to something, but she wasn't sure if she had the time to figure out what it might be. If Brad got the loan from the bank before she could, he'd get the farm. "How long would you stay for?"

"Maybe a night or two." His smugness snapped across the line. He always sounded like that when he knew he was close to closing the deal. She wanted to say forget it, that she didn't need his money after all, but she clamped her lips down to stop the vomit of words ready to spew.

"You can't stay with me." She could control at least that much.

"Why not?"

Because the guest room was already filled, and because she didn't want him sleeping anywhere near her any longer.

"It's not a good idea for us to share living space, Oliver. I can't have that."

"Do you hate me that much?"

"No, I just don't want to live through you recoiling every time I come near you." She also didn't want to be the one who jumped away at the idea he might touch her. Because she would be that one now. After having Caleb holding her, she might not ever want another man to touch her that way. They had only lain together, but it had been more intimate and safer than anything she had had with Oliver.

"I don't do that." He almost sounded horrified. She tried not to laugh.

"If I agree to allow you to visit the farm, does that mean you'll lend me the money?" She needed to stay focused on her goal. Once she got the money, she wouldn't have to deal with him other than to send a check each month. She could still handle sending a check in an envelope. Or better, she could transfer the money over an app.

"The visit by itself isn't enough to convince me. I want to see what your plans are for the business. I'm not about to lose tens of thousands of dollars because you don't have a business plan."

"Fine. Can you come in a couple of weeks?" She would rather Caleb be long gone by the time Oliver got here. His bike would be done by then. No matter what she felt with Caleb's arms around her, he wouldn't stay in town. She couldn't blame him. Too many people whispered when he went by. The town couldn't wait to mull over his appearance at her farm. She wished it could be different, but it would never be.

"I suspect you want the money sooner than later," Oliver said.

"Yes. As soon as possible."

"Then I'll be there in two days." He ended the call.

CHAPTER EIGHT

Brooklyn covered her ears. Lucy the two-toned beige alpaca wouldn't stop screeching. Two of the boys, Chewpaca and Alistair ran in circles tooting. She didn't know what to do, and she needed to do it fast before Alpacino hurt himself.

"Stop screaming," she said to Lucy, as if the alpaca could be reasoned with. Lucy didn't understand her, and if she did, she didn't care. Lucy was her good Samaritan always calling for help in times of stress.

"Everything okay, here?" Caleb appeared around the side of the barn. She sighed at the sight of him in his long-sleeve Henley that melted to the curves of his torso and snug-fitting jeans. His smile lit up his face which was healing nicely from the accident. His limp was almost gone too. She enjoyed this older version of him even if his frown lines were deeper than the smile lines.

"Boy, am I glad to see you. Alpacino is stuck. I can't lift the rail above his head by myself. I'm also not sure how to get his head through the wire fence." The poor alpaca had tried to scurry under the fence where the wood rail had collapsed and broke open the wiring. Last time the rail had fallen, the hole was big enough for him to squeeze through, and he did. He had wandered over to the winery and scared the hell out of Weezer River, almost getting himself shot in the process.

"Let's do it together." He strode over to Alpacino who struggled against the rail and made sounds like a high-pitched motor. "Hey, boy. It's okay. I'm going to cut the wire fencing."

"But that will leave a permanent hole that I can't have today. It's my lunch with the alpacas this afternoon. I'll be worried all day that someone will get out."

"I'll take care of the wiring and fix the wood rail so it won't fall and rip the wire like it did last time. Don't panic." He beamed another smile at her that calmed the storm in her stomach a little. He seemed content here at the farm or maybe that was her imagination.

"Am I panicking? Yes, okay. I am. It's my first event without Cordy." And may very well be her last. She needed this to go well to prove to herself and to everyone else she could handle running this farm.

Caleb pulled out a pocketknife and flipped open the blade. She jumped. The silver glinted against the sun's rays. The blade was long and pointed with a serrated edge. A look of confusion crossed his face as he looked at her, but he tended to Alpacino without questioning why she had recoiled like a shotgun. Slicing through the wire as if it were butter, he pushed Alpacino's head through the hole with ease. He flipped the blade shut and shoved the knife back in his pocket without breaking a sweat.

"You need to stay out of that fence, buddy, or you're going to hurt yourself. We can't have that," Caleb said, petting Alpacino who hummed in response. Caleb turned to her. "You're going to be fine. You're a natural with the animals, and you're a nurse. You know how to talk to people."

"I was a nurse, and I'm not sure how well I spoke to my patients. I'd like to think I was a calming force for them, but delivering instructions was my primary responsibility." She had to make sure they knew how to take care of themselves or a loved one when they left her care. After the attack, when she couldn't address their needs because she found herself hiding in the bathroom shaking from the memories of what had happened to her, she had known it was time to go.

"You don't give yourself enough credit. You took good care of me when I showed up on your doorstep all busted up."

She hadn't stopped to think about her problems when she opened the door to him. He was familiar—and most importantly, hurt. Her instincts had kicked in, but she couldn't be sure they would always appear when she needed them. Nursing was a thing of the past for her, but if she could keep the farm, taking care of the alpacas would be a nice replacement.

"I also showed up at the door with a gun." That had been the first time she had ever done anything like that. The gun had given her power she hadn't felt. She would ask Cordy to teach her how to use it properly when she came home, just as a safety measure.

"Where I come from, when a stranger shows up at your door in the middle of the night, having a gun handy is smart. Why don't you go do whatever you still need to do for the lunch today? I'll take care of the animals and fix the fence. I can also set up the tables and chairs if you want. I'll even clean their bathroom spot."

"You would do all that for me?" She wasn't used to the help. Her ex-husband often begged off chores with excuses of having to work. She would pull a twelve-hour shift at the hospital only to come home and have to cook and clean and do the laundry.

"Of course. Why wouldn't I?" He smirked as if she had said something preposterous.

Alistair waddled over and dropped the rake he carried under his neck. Caleb bent to grab it, but Alistair snagged it and ran away. Caleb let out a hearty laugh.

"Alistair, you're the man," Caleb said.

Her insides glowed like tonic water under black light. He loved the alpacas. A man who cared for animals was not a killer. "Doing all that work around here is a lot to ask of you." Having him work on the farm wasn't a part of their original agreement to have him stay, but she liked the idea of sharing tasks with him.

"You're not asking me. I'm offering because I want to, and because you're giving me a place to crash until my bike is fixed. The least I can do is help you out around here."

"But you paid me rent." Money that she had shoved into a jar and added to her down payment fund like a teenager saving for her first car.

He moved closer and placed a hand on her shoulder. His warmth consumed her. "I want to help you because you're one of the few people who have been kind to me. When you look at me, you don't see a killer."

"That's because you're not." She stared into his penetrating eyes, not wanting to look away.

"I wish everyone thought the way you do."

"They would if they knew you like I do." He had never been angry or violent with her, but anyone could snap in a second and he could become a man capable of hitting her. But when she pushed fear away, her heart told her he wasn't that man. He had only ever stood up for himself because he had no one else to do it for him.

Her mouth dried and her words grated against her tight

throat. She caught a whiff of his masculine scent mixed with the smell of hay. Her body's response to him was ridiculous. He wasn't interested in her that way anymore. He was just helping with a few chores.

But the ease in her chest when he was near hadn't been there before he showed up here. She hadn't expected him to bring her any peace. She had just been offering him a place to heal, but his self-assured swagger and his ability to handle whatever was thrown at him, settled comfort over her like a warm blanket.

"I'm not the same man I was when we were together." They hadn't spoken of that time since his return. At first it seemed like an unwritten rule between them. Leave the past in the past and all that. But his presence had brought back many memories. Nice memories of his kindness and caring, and his attentiveness toward her in a way no one would believe the rowdy and edgy Caleb Ransom was capable of. She wondered what he thought of their short time together back then. If he had revisited it at all over the years.

"I can see your heart, Caleb." It was as if the ground shifted under her. What was she doing here with this man? She wasn't sure, but she wanted the time to find out, wanted him to stay longer. Her heart cracked open a little. The new embrasure needed to be explored.

"How can you see that?" His voice dropped lower. His lids were hooded.

"When I look in your eyes, your heart is there. The way you held me the other night while I was frightened. Your touch was gentle and protective."

"You were always better with words than me." He brushed her hair away from her face. "What is this scar from?" He leaned in to get a closer look.

Her hand instinctively came up and covered it. He backed up. "An accident last year."

"I'm sorry you were in an accident. Was it a car accident?"

"No, nothing like that." The truth lingered on her lips, but she didn't say it.

"May I touch you there?"

She swallowed and nodded. Oliver had never wanted to touch her scar. Caleb lightly ran the pad of his finger over the place her attacker had cut her. "It's beautiful."

"Oh, please." She choked out a laugh.

"I'm serious. It's a part of you. Nothing that is a part of you could be bad."

"I don't know about that," she said.

"I do." His confident smile returned. Her heart ached to believe that smile.

He ran his hand up and down her arm, his touch gentle. Her skin tingled with each stroke. The words to ask for more from him formed in her brain, but her mouth clamped them down. She and Caleb were too new, and she didn't have men touch her anymore. Not intimately, anyway. But the thoughts of him pressed against her edged foreword in her mind, wanting to take hold.

"You're not the only one who has changed. I'm not the same person either." She was damaged and broken. She may never be whole again, but she wanted to try… She wanted to try, if only to remember what pleasure against her skin could do to her.

"I wouldn't expect you to be the same. We're older. We've lived lives that aren't always easy. I don't care about your past. All I care about is what's happening right here." He eased closer, stopping to run his finger along her scar again. "May I kiss you?" His thumb caressed her bottom lip.

She stifled a sob. He had asked first. He must know some-how. But how? Could he read her mind? Standing on the farm, her favorite place, with the alpacas playing nearby, she nodded her consent.

He brought his lips to hers. They were soft, and they didn't pry. She held her breath as the pressure of his kiss increased and willed her body to relax. He rested his hands on either side of her face, in a gentle way, giving her time to adjust.

"I can stop if you want me to." He kissed her cheek then moved his lips to her neck.

"Don't stop." Her words were barely audible.

His lips followed the scar down and then up. Her whole body awakened like a new day. He wrapped his arms around her waist and pulled her closer. She reached around his neck and relaxed into him. Wanting more, she opened her mouth to his. He took her invitation, spinning her world on its head. The kiss curled her toes. She tangled her fingers in his hair. His hands slid over her back.

He eased away before she was ready to end things. Heat flowed in waves over her body as if she were a volcano that had lain dormant for a long time. His smile covered her with a bright light.

"Was that okay?" he said.

Her fingers touched his lips. They were wet and swollen. He took her hand and kissed her palm. Her legs trembled from the rush of it all. She needed to sit before she fell on her butt and really embarrassed herself.

"I never expected to be kissing you when I woke up this morning." But she had thought about it, if she were going to be honest.

"I've wanted to kiss you since you asked me to sleep with you the other night."

She had wanted him next to her, holding her. Caleb had a way of making her feel undamaged, which was crazy because they hadn't seen each other in ten years. She had no idea what he had been up to in that time. How much had prison changed him? Because it had to have. How could it not?

This was all too much. Her mind screamed to slow down, that she was taking too big a risk by even considering being sexual with Caleb. The problem was her body wanted his hands on it, touching, exploring. She wanted to find out what he was like in bed now. She wanted to make love to a man for the first time in more than a year. This man.

"Could we talk about this some more tonight? I have that lunch." She was running scared like those times at the hospital. She didn't know how to tell him about what happened to her and didn't want to see the look in his eyes change when she did. When she was younger, and before her attack, she could afford to be more daring, but not now.

He stepped aside. "Sure. No problem. I'll take care of the animals and the fence. You're going to have a good day."

"Thanks." She hurried off, afraid to look over her shoulder. She might turn on her heel and run into his arms. She couldn't allow that to happen. He was leaving soon, and she wanted to stay. He was uncertainty and confusion. She needed a strong foundation under her right now.

Not wanting to think about Caleb's hands and what they could do to her, she busied herself with getting ready for the lunch with alpacas event. She swept the porch and the walkway. She watered the orange and yellow mums. Customers didn't come inside the house, but Cordy wanted the outside to look welcoming. Brooklyn had hung cornstalks on the porch's posts and had a large basket of apples from the orchard.

Above the alpaca barn was the small shop where Cordy sold her goods. Brooklyn made sure the hats, scarves, gloves, and blankets were stocked in a variety of colors. Their inventory was running low. She would need to start knitting, if she was going to make this business work. Cordy was going to take her skills and go soon. She wouldn't be able to afford to send out all the yarn to a production place to make the items. And the customers enjoyed the fact Cordy's merchandise was handmade. It's what made her goods and her special. Her heart ached, knowing her grandmother would be on the other side of the country soon. She didn't know what she would do without her.

She cleaned the small bathroom in the gift shop that customers could use and made sure there was bottled water in the metal bucket by the register along with some of the yarn they sold for other people to knit with.

Back inside the house, she took a quick shower and changed into a clean pair of jeans and a flannel shirt. Ten families had booked the lunch with the alpacas today. Cordy held this event once a month and people came for miles. The lunch was catered by the orchard, which made the food part easy to handle since she wasn't much of a cook. Her cousin Annabelle had dropped off the boxed lunches this morning. All Brooklyn had to do was help the people say hello to the alpacas. Take some pictures. And keep her lips off Caleb.

Brooklyn pushed outside and took a cleansing breath. The smell of hay and honeysuckle lingered in the air. The afternoon was the kind a bride might hope for on her wedding day. The sun was bright, but the crisp fall air made it cool enough in the shade for a jacket. The colors on the trees were at their most vibrant before their descent into a withered brown and blown from the trees until spring.

Cordy's one employee, Malinda, was already directing cars to the parking spots. Brooklyn did a quick search for Caleb. He was over at the fence. The alpacas ambled around their barn. Alistair still had the rake. She put a leash on Ethel, the only other female, to be able to direct her to any of the kids who were too shy to come into the barn.

She handed out the boxed lunches and encouraged families to say hello to the animals by giving them small bags of alpaca food. The event basically ran itself. Caleb gave her a wave and went inside the house.

"I'm going up to the store. I want to be there when people are ready to buy," Malinda said. She brushed her corkscrew hair away from her flawless face.

"How do you think the event is going?"

"Like a charm. Cordy would be proud. You're really doing a great job with them, Brooklyn. Cordy isn't going to need me soon."

"You aren't thinking of leaving, are you?" She hoped Malinda would stay on after Cordy sold and moved away. Assuming she got the farm over Brad. If Brad became the new owner, Malinda would be out of job anyway.

"No way. Not unless I hit the lottery or my aunt Betty dies." She tilted her head back, laughed with gusto, and slapped her leg. The bracelets on her thin arm jangled in response.

"I'm glad to hear that." Gladder than Malinda could know.

Brooklyn moved from group to group introducing herself. Many people asked for Cordy. Her grandmother was a staple in this town. The place wouldn't be the same when she moved. Brooklyn wouldn't be the same either.

She approached a couple sitting at one of the picnic benches. The man, she assumed the husband based on the classic gray wedding band on his left hand, held a baby girl in his lap. She couldn't be more than a year old, but she laughed and shoved her fists in her mouth each time her daddy bounced her on his leg. The man looked down on his daughter in awe. The woman sat opposite this breathtaking sight and held up her cell phone to snap pictures.

"Lyanna, look at Mommy." The woman waved toward the baby.

"Babe, she doesn't know what you're saying." The man

took the baby's hand and waved it toward the camera. "Let's wave at Mommy so we can eat our lunch before your second birthday." He barked out a laugh.

"Hawk Egan, you're impossible."

He beamed at his wife. Brooklyn took in the sight of this family, and her breath stuck in her lungs. When she had married Oliver, she believed she would have a family of her own and get a chance to become the kind of mother hers wasn't. But time had a way of moving at a hare's pace, and Oliver always had something he wanted to accomplish first. Now she was almost forty and may have missed her chance. For good.

"I don't mean to interrupt, but I wanted to make sure you had everything you needed," she said.

"We're fine. Thank you," the man called Hawk said.

"We are having a great time. The alpacas are so sweet and your farm is beautiful." The woman scooted off the bench and stuck out her hand. "I'm Aria Scirocco-Egan and this is my husband Hawk and our daughter Lyanna."

"It's very nice to meet you all."

Hawk gave her a half salute. Lyanna gifted her another juicy laugh. Her heart wanted to leap out of her chest.

"I'm a wedding planner down at the shore. Do you hold weddings here?" Aria said.

"We just have the alpacas and the monthly lunch."

"This would be a fantastic location for a rustic-themed wedding. Brides love the photo opportunities inside a barn or out in the field. You could even offer up the alpacas to be a part of the special day." Aria's face lit up when she spoke.

"I don't think my grandmother ever considered hosting weddings." Cordy wasn't much of a planner. Trying to coordinate brides and photo shoots weren't exactly her strong suit.

"Oh, she should. You could bring in business without a lot of overhead. Just a few adjustments on the farm for photo opportunities. Right here where we're having lunch, under this canopy of trees would be a beautiful spot to set up tables. Take my card." Aria dug in her oversized tote and handed her a business card. "I would love to talk to you more about this. I could bring couples by to see the place. You could even offer engagement photos here. The space just goes on and on. I love the rolling hills."

"It's very pretty here. I agree. I'll speak to my grandmother about it. Thanks." She tapped the business card.

"Great. I'll be in touch," Aria said.

"Enjoy the rest of the day. Bye, Lyanna." She waved to the beautiful baby.

"Lyanna, wave goodbye to the nice lady." Hawk lifted his daughter's hand and waved again. "Oh, I didn't get your name." Aria grabbed her phone and swiped at the screen. "I'll just put the farm in my contacts."

"Brooklyn. Brooklyn Wilde."

"Well, Brooklyn, I could keep this place very busy if you'll let me."

"Babe, let the woman go talk to other guests." Hawk smiled at his wife again without any malice in his voice. The guy was clearly in love. No one had ever looked at her as if she had hung the moon.

"I'm sorry. I just get so excited." Aria blushed.

"Don't be. I'll keep in touch too." And she would.

Brooklyn stood off to the side and soaked in her surroundings. Hosting weddings at the farm would be another source of revenue for her. She'd have to check into the details, but it could be worth it. She loved the idea of bringing happy people here to share in their special day. She needed more joy in her life than anguish. Brides and grooms were generally happy. The new venture would be something she could tell Oliver about when he arrived. Hopefully, that would help convince him she was a good investment. She still needed to talk to Brad about what she was attempting. She needed him to back off and let her have this. She had no backup plan if he didn't. Maybe Caleb would let her hitch a ride with him to his next stop, if the farm fell through.

Guests made their way to the store. Others interacted with the alpacas, taking pictures filled with laughter. Some guests sat under a tree and enjoyed their lunch. She had been worried this day would end badly. That something during the lunch would go wrong. Other than Alpacino getting stuck in the fence, she had made a success of the event. She could prove to her grandmother she could handle what happened at the farm.

"Looks like the day is going better than you thought." Caleb appeared alongside her like an apparition. His musky smell mingled with the scent of hay and freshly cut grass that lingered in the air.

"Surprisingly so." She tucked Aria's business card into her back pocket.

"I knew it would. You belong here." His fingers grazed hers. A faint echo of desire spread over her. "Have you figured out a way to get the money?" he said.

"My ex-husband might lend it to me." She couldn't meet his gaze because at her age she should be able to get a loan from a bank. She hadn't been very good at saving money. Growing up in a sparse cabin had made her long for nice things in her younger years. She had become someone who had racked up credit card debt. She was a little too much like her mother.

Having to admit to Caleb she needed her ex was a tough pill to swallow. She stared off at the couple she had just met, Hawk and Aria, who fed Lucy some hay. What that family shared was far more important than material things. The last year had shown her that.

"Your ex? Is he a good guy?"

"He's good with money and happens to have plenty of it. I don't have any other options on such short notice." Oliver wasn't all bad. She believed he had truly loved her in the beginning, the best way he could. But his career had become more important. He wanted all the things money could buy. He thought his success was wrapped up in the big house, the fast car, the designer suits. She had grown tired of his pursuit of objects long before her attack. If she wanted to find a silver lining in the worst thing that ever happened to her, it was finally admitting she and Oliver were wrong for each other.

"I wish I could give you the money. I wouldn't lend it either. I'm not some damn bank. I'd give it to you because you deserve to have your dreams come true."

The passion in his voice shook her. "I wouldn't let you give me that much money, but thank you. What you just said was probably the nicest thing anyone has ever said to me." She had always wanted a man in her life who would help her make her dreams come true. Oliver was not that man.

But Caleb with his intense eyes that seemed to look right through her and that set jaw as if he were determined to see her plan through, could he be that man? Her hand reached for her scar. She couldn't allow herself to think too much more about what Caleb had said. He wasn't going to be in town long enough to make anything happen for her. But it was still nice to hear. He had soothed some of her frayed edges.

"Hey, can I ask you something?" His voice dragged her away from her thoughts.

"Sure." She would accept an invitation to dinner or a long walk by moonlight. She would allow him to sit by the fire with her, drink some wine, and remind her how to feel like a woman.

"Would it be all right if I borrow your car? I wanted to go into town and get some groceries."

She stifled a groan and hoped the heat on her cheeks didn't give her away. Not the question she expected. "No problem. The keys are hanging by the door."

He placed a soft kiss by her ear and lingered. His warm breath sent shivers over her skin. "I'll ask a better question next time."

CHAPTER NINE

Caleb wanted to make dinner for Brooklyn as a way to say thank you for letting him stay at her place, and because he wanted to spend time with her. He wasn't expecting anything, but if she wanted to take that earlier kiss further, he would oblige her.

His first stop was the Rivers Edge Winery. Weezer River had always believed in his innocence, which he appreciated. He had also wanted to say hello to his old friend Malbec. Like him, Malbec had made an unexpected visit to Candlewood Falls.

He stood inside the winery's gift shop while Malbec searched for a wine. The old wood barn structure was pretty much the same since the last time he was here, with its high rafters and its smell of fermented grapes and sawdust, but the years had rubbed away some of the luster.

"This is a good year, and a fine blend, unless you're having fish. Then I'd go for a white," Malbec said, handing him a merlot.

"This will work. Thanks." He dug out his wallet and paid. They talked a little more, but he was ready to get to the supermarket. After all the work on the farm earlier, his body ached. He would need a hot shower before he made dinner or he would be hunched over like an old man.

He turned to go, but stopped. A crazy idea flashed through his mind. One he would not have considered if he and Malbec hadn't been good friends once. They had hung out at school and when they were kids, the Rivers had taken him on their family vacations. That was something his own family could never do.

"Hey, Malbec?"

"Yeah?"

"Any chance the winery is hiring? Like I said, I'm leaving town, but if my plans change and I stick around...would you need any help?"

"Man, I would hire you in a second. So would my mother. But I don't know what's happening with the winery. If it sells quickly, you might find yourself out of work. I can't do that to you. See if you can't find something else first."

"Sure. Thanks." He saluted with the wine. "Tell Merlot I said hello." The disappointment surprised him. He wasn't even planning on staying in town...but if things continued with Brooklyn. He shook the thoughts away. He wasn't staying, and Malbec was being a friend by saving his pride. There was no reason to hire him.

"Will do. He asks about you all the time."

He nodded and pushed through the door. Merlot River had become a parole officer because Caleb had been wrongly accused. Merlot wanted to make sure people who cared and couldn't be bought worked with the prisoners when they were released. The River family were full of good people. Too bad the winery might not remain theirs.

He headed to the supermarket and walked up and down every aisle trying to decide what to make for Brooklyn. He couldn't remember the last time the idea of eating with a woman churned excitement in his belly. Now he was anxious to get home. *Home.* He needed to be careful. The alpaca farm was anything but home at the moment, but being with Brooklyn made it feel a little more like it.

Leaving the supermarket with more groceries than he had planned to buy, he pushed the cart through the empty parking lot. Only a few lonely cars dotted some spots and those were in the shadows. The extra time he had spent in the store allowed the sun to dip out of the sky and cast a dull gray over everything around him.

A wind had picked up and shoved its way under his jacket and chilled the scrapes on his skin still healing from the accident. The fierce gusts forced a vagrant shopping cart across the asphalt, its metal wheels clanking in pain along the way.

He dug his keys out of his pocket and dropped them. He almost laughed at himself for being slightly nervous about this dinner.

He couldn't decide what to make, but he had chosen pasta and ingredients for a quick but spicy tomato sauce. Nothing too special, just a meal that offered comfort. She was trusting him, and he wanted to encourage that more. He liked being wanted.

Popping the trunk to load the groceries, something grabbed his shoulders hard and spun him around. The bag slipped from his hand and glass shattered against the pavement. The pain to his face was instant. The blow to his stomach bent him in half and knocked all the wind out of him. He tried to fight back, but someone kicked out his knee, and he hit the ground, pebbles scraped his cheek. His instincts had him protecting his face while the kicks came. Two guys maybe three. Just like in prison. He wouldn't be able to get up before they killed him. The men grunted with each swing of their legs.

He dared to open an eye. A piece of glass from the tomato

sauce jar glinted in the parking lot light like a beacon. He grabbed it and sliced the calf of one of his assailants. The man screamed out in pain.

"That's enough. Leave him be now." Another man's familiar voice came from somewhere behind him, but he didn't risk looking to see where or who he was. But he wasn't one of the ones kicking him. That much he was sure of because the voice was too far away.

The kicking stopped, but the pain pulsated over his body. His lungs struggled to suck in air.

"Get the hell out of this town. A murderer that looks like you doesn't belong here," said a different, maybe third, man. He didn't recognize the voice at all. "If I find you alone next time, you won't be so lucky." The man spit on him.

"Let's go now," the familiar voice said, the first one who had spoken. Where had he heard that voice before? "You'd do yourself a favor by packing it up. That woman you're staying with is going to get hurt because of you."

Feet pounded the pavement, running away from him. A car engine started somewhere in the distance. He had to get to Brooklyn and make sure she was safe. He counted to ten before he tried to stand.

And fell back down.

Brooklyn closed the front door and was alone. Finally. The day had been a big success, but long and stressful. After the last guest had left, she fed the alpacas and brushed them. Chewpaca had snuggled up against her. She loved petting his gray and tan fleece. She had snapped a few pictures of her smiling alpacas, but before she could get inside and post them online, Mrs. Holloway had appeared in the driveway with a cake.

She had wanted to thank Brooklyn for the banana bread. She has also wanted to get a look at Caleb. She had given the police sketch artist a description of the person who had beaten her. Based on what Mrs. Holloway could remember, that man could be anyone. Including Caleb.

"Do you have a picture of him, dear?" Mrs. H had said.

"I don't. I'm sorry." And if she did, she wasn't going to share it and give Mrs. H any ideas.

"When will he be back?"

"I thought he would be back by now." And she had. He was gone far longer than he should be if he were only picking up a few groceries. They were going to have dinner together, and she was looking forward to it.

"I want to see if he looks like the man I saw." Mrs. Holloway hadn't taken the hints Brooklyn had tried to give so she could go inside and clean up, but she hadn't had the heart to tell the old woman she was tired and wanted to take a hot bath before Caleb returned. She wanted to get the barn smell out of her hair and put on something pretty.

Now, she leaned against the inside of the front door and wiped her hands over her face. Oliver would be here tomorrow. As much as she didn't want him around—what she did was none of Oliver's business—she did want him to lend her the money. She didn't want to have to explain who Caleb was, but Oliver was sure to ask questions about the man in the house.

Cordy would return the following day. Maybe a house full of people would convince Oliver nothing was going on between her and Caleb. Besides, there wasn't really. That kiss didn't mean anything. Well, it meant something to her. That kiss meant the chance to live a little.

Lucy started her warning screech. Someone was on the property. Tires crunched over the gravel. A fieriness spread over her belly. Caleb had returned. The car door slammed.

She hesitated before opening the front door. She didn't want to seem too anxious, as if she were watching and waiting by the window. Instead, she ran into the kitchen and searched for a bottle of wine, but found none. The front door opened before she could close the cabinet.

She took a deep breath, smoothed her hair, and made her way back into the living room. A scream formed on her lips, but she stifled it in time. Caleb swayed before her as if the floor tilted under him. He steadied himself with the arm of the couch and attempted to smile, but his cheek had swollen on one side, making his top lip immobile. Both of his eyes were blood shot and rimmed with black circles. The gash on his forehead leaked blood in a thin line. His clothes were dirty. A shoeprint was on his shirt.

"What happened?" She ran to his side.

"Are you okay?" He tangled his fingers in her hair, cupping her head. He searched her gaze with his glassy one.

"Me? Look at you. Who did this?" She took his hands and led him to the sofa, helping him sit. "Stay put." She ran, once again, to get supplies to clean him up. He was bleeding from scrapes on his face. His hand was covered in blood. It looked as if he sliced his palm, from what she could tell in one quick glance. The wound could need stitches. She returned with a determination to get to the bottom of this.

"I'm fine. I wanted to make sure you're okay." He waved away the damp cloth.

"Why wouldn't I be okay?" He wasn't making any sense. He must've taken a hard hit to the head.

"Because of me." His head bobbed on his neck.

"Do you feel like you're going to pass out?" She checked his pulse, but it wasn't erratic.

"No. I'm okay. As long as you're safe, I'm fine."

"What are you getting at?" She lifted the hem of his shirt, wanting to see if there was more damage to his torso.

"Why are you pulling on my shirt? Is this foreplay?" He winked, but it turned into a wince instead.

"I need to see where you're hurt. Can you take off your shirt?" She held her hand out. He struggled to pull the fabric over his head. "I suppose a visit to the ER is out of the question?"

"I'm okay, really. Just a little banged up. The groceries didn't make it home. I'm sorry. I've ruined the dinner plans."

"Never mind that. Let me check you out." She looked for signs of a concussion, but none were present. His ribs were bruised again, maybe even a hairline fracture. His wrist could be sprained, and his palm would benefit from some stitches. "Please let me take you somewhere to stitch this up."

"Just use an extra bandage." He used his shirt to blot at the cut on his palm which was starting to clot on the edge.

"You're crazy. What if I've missed something? What if you're bleeding internally? I can't know that without a scan." He needed tests done to rule out any major problems.

"I'll tell you if I need the hospital, okay?"

"Short of throwing you over my shoulder, do I have much choice but to take your word you're okay?" He was as stubborn as he was gentle. He hated hospitals and doctors. She would not win this argument. She only hoped she didn't regret not fighting harder.

"Which you won't do." He teased her with a lopsided smile.

"Don't tempt me." She finished cleaning him up and wrapping his injuries the best she could with what she had. "Are you going to tell me what happened?"

"Come sit next to me." He patted the spot beside him.

She sat in the corner of the sofa, keeping some distance between her and his bare chest. "Spill it."

"I was jumped."

"What? By whom? Where?"

He closed his eyes and leaned his head back. "I don't know. There were three or four of them. One sounded old. I'm pretty sure he wasn't involved in the beating. They told me they wanted me out of town. That I didn't belong here. Same story I always hear when I'm in town. No one wants me dirtying up their neighborhood."

The hairs on the back of her neck stood up. Her uncle Huck was the president of the Brotherhood of Watchmen, a local group of narrow-minded men who had a sick definition of who belonged and who didn't and often vocalized it. They pretended to be a neighborhood group of men who were concerned about the safety and well-being of the residents of Candlewood Falls, but they bullied anyone who was different from them. They had been known to run a few people out of town, but they also had a reputation for taking what they wanted in any means necessary. The police's hands were tied because no crime had actually been connected to the Watchmen. And some say because they had an insider in the group.

"I need to run out. Stay here." She jumped up, but his viselike grip clamped down on her wrist.

"Please don't go anywhere. Not tonight." He released her.

"I want to talk to my father." She could try and call his cell, but he so rarely answered it. She needed her father's help. He was the only person who could call Huck and his men off Caleb. If it had been his men, but who else could it be? Even those that disliked Caleb wouldn't go to such lengths.

"I don't think your father is going to want to help me. He's already made it perfectly clear he doesn't want me here either. In the morning, I'm going to take my bike, fixed or not, and find another town to heal up in. Then I'll be on the road and away from you. I don't want you to get hurt because of me." He pushed off the couch but stopped halfway to standing. Pain crossed his face, and he pushed air out through his teeth.

"You should leave town because I don't want you to keep getting hurt. The next time you might not be so lucky. But you will not allow those men to run you out of here. You did nothing wrong. You deserve to be here as much as I do." She couldn't just sit there and watch him suffer in pain. She tried to help him stand to his full height, but he waved her away.

"Yeah? How are you going to convince them I belong? You're nothing more than a little thing. They could snap you in two, and I won't allow that to happen. You don't need my mess stinking you up. You have a real chance to make a life here. It's what you want, and I want you to have that." He limped away.

It was her turn to grip his wrist, but she made sure to grab the healthy one. "You don't have to protect me." Though she liked the idea of it. After the attack, she had wanted to be with someone who tamed the fear. Even now, she wished she had someone lying beside her at night. She didn't want to be alone in the dark. She would've stayed with Oliver if he hadn't been disgusted by her, which would've been a mistake. The someone she wanted was Caleb.

"I think I do have to keep you safe. Without meaning to, I made it my job. If one of those men lays a hand on you, I will go to jail for murder this time. And I'd be happy for it."

"No one is coming for me. I'm a Wilde. My entire family would be on the hunt for someone trying to hurt me. Even my uncle Huck can't be stupid enough to put me in harm's way because I care about you."

"Brooks, I can't stay here knowing I'm the thing causing you trouble."

"You don't have to make me your responsibility. I can take care of myself." What would she do when he left town? Who would protect her heart then? Because that was what needed protecting.

"I know you can, but that doesn't mean I don't want to. I'll fight anyone to keep you safe."

"Don't use your fists to protect me, okay? I don't want you fighting." She wouldn't be able to stand it if anything bad happened to him. He was lucky tonight. He might not be so lucky in the future, and she couldn't watch that happen.

He ran his thumb over her chin. "I won't promise that. No one is going to hurt you ever on my watch."

"I don't want you to go." She liked having him there, but they both knew he wasn't staying. All his promises were well-intended, but he wasn't safe in town. "But I understand why you have to leave. Officer Vetter is gunning for you, and now you have a group of men trying to kill you. What's in it for you to stay? If I were you, I'd go too."

"What's in it for me?"

"Yes. What could be so great about Candlewood Falls that for the first time in twelve years you would want to stick around when your life is in danger?"

He stared at her with something forcible passing over his eyes. "You want to know why I'm staying?"

"Yes. Is that such a hard question?"

"What's keeping me here is you, Brooklyn. You."

CHAPTER TEN

Caleb couldn't sleep. The pain from the last beating pulsed along the side of his body. No position on the soft mattress could keep the jagged edges of discomfort away. He had downed some ibuprofen, but it wasn't enough. And he had meant what he said. No doctors or hospitals. He preferred to take care of himself unless he was without any other options. Even the prison infirmary had proven to be less than safe. Danger lurked everywhere in that place. That was why he needed to stay one step ahead. His time in Candlewood Falls was up. Sticking around much longer would land him in a coffin. Never mind a hospital.

He threw back the covers and paced at frustratingly slow speed. He really needed to pay better attention to his surroundings. He knew better. That was how he had stayed alive in prison, by keeping his eye on his enemies. And that was everyone. He hadn't joined any of the groups who had promised protection because that protection came with a price he wasn't willing to pay. That also meant he was on his own in a world where you needed someone watching your back. The two years had been the hardest of his life. If he ever had to return, he'd end his life first. He couldn't allow Officer Vetter to pin the assault and robbery on him. The only way he could see fit to do that was to leave. Vetter had no proof. That poor excuse for a cop only had hatred for him.

But he had told Brooklyn he wanted to stay for her. Stay in Candlewood Falls? The bedroom closed in on him, snuffing all the air out. He needed space and the open road with no destination in mind. He needed the power of his motorcycle between his legs, but he also wanted Brooklyn's soft body beneath him. He ran his hands over his face. Thoughts like that had no place in his mind.

A stiff drink might help ease some of the pain and get him off to sleep without any more images of Brooklyn. He hoped she had something stronger than wine in the house. He hadn't seen anything that fit that description since he arrived, but maybe he had missed it.

He opened the bedroom door. A soft light filtered down the hall. The sounds of quiet movement, shuffling and cabinets closing on a subtle click, drifted in his direction. Brooklyn must be up too. He hesitated at the entrance to the kitchen, not wanting to scare her, but also wanting to watch her. She stood with her back to him. Her t-shirt hung just below her backside and exposed her toned legs and bare feet. Her hair fell down her back in waves. He wanted to run his hands through it again. Even now, his skin remembered the silky strands wrapped around his fingers when he grabbed her earlier. Heat traveled south. She was the most beautiful woman he ever saw. And she had been his once for a short time.

"You couldn't sleep either?" he said.

She jumped and spun around, her eyes growing to the size of tires. She clasped the collar of her shirt. "I didn't see you there."

"I'm sorry I scared you. I didn't mean to." He approached

her the way he might approach a frightened bird. She seemed ready to take off without warning. She had tried to hide the nerves, the worried glances, and the reason for the night-mare, but he was used to watching people. Paying attention had started a long time ago, when he was a child and needed to keep himself safe. Now it was a habit.

"It's okay." She turned back to the counter. "I was making tea. Do you want some?"

"No, thanks. Not much of a tea drinker."

"Why? You're too much of a man for tea?" She dunked the bag in and out of the mug. Her smile tugged at the corners of her full mouth. A playfulness dashed across her eyes.

He choked out a laugh. "Something like that. What has you up at this hour?"

"You're missing out on some really good chamomile." She dropped into the chair and tucked her legs under her. She kept her gaze on her mug. "I had a bad dream again."

"But not like the last one." He would have heard the screams, if it had been. He grabbed the seat next to hers. Her clean scent mixed with the spices of the tea and settled against him.

"I guess not."

"What is the dream about?" He wanted to know what had this woman so torn up. Was it the ex-husband who would be coming to visit her? He doubted it had anything to do with her family. The Wildes were a tight-knit group who loved each other. No matter what he thought of Brad, he knew Brad cared for his sister and only wanted the best for her.

"I really don't want to talk about it." She sipped the tea.

"Maybe you should."

"Because you think if I do, the nightmares will stop? I've already tried that. Six months of therapy and nothing. I've tried CBD oil, sleeping pills which made me feel groggy and gross, and even acupuncture. Nothing helps. You don't have to make any more suggestions."

He raised his hands in surrender. "Only trying to help."

"I know. I'm sorry. It's just you're a man, and men usually want to solve the problem and move on. I don't need a problem solver at the moment."

"I won't deny that you pretty much described me, but I have never had the luxury of dwelling on my problems for long. If I didn't fix them, no one else would." With the exception of his mother helping him get out of prison.

"Are you saying I'm hanging onto something I shouldn't be?" She placed the mug on the table with force. The tea spilled over the top. "Shit. Look what I did." She sprang up and grabbed some paper towels to clean the mess.

"I wasn't implying you should let your problems go." He stood and took the towels from her, expecting her to argue with him about him trying to take over. "Let me. Sit down."

She stared up, only inches from him. She had a tiny freckle on the top of her lip. The space between them sizzled with heat. His hand remained over her smaller one, as if it was meant to be there. And maybe it was because he didn't want to pull away.

"The nightmares are because I don't feel safe. Except since you've been here. After that first one, I haven't had any so bad I wake up screaming." Her words whispered against his skin like a gentle touch.

"I make you feel safe?" He wasn't expecting her to say that. Even though he suspected how she felt, he wasn't sure she knew it with any clarity.

"Does that surprise you?" she said as if she had read his mind.

"Some." He wanted to stop all the talking and kiss her again. A full kiss where he could taste her, but he held back.

"Caleb..." She stared at him without another word, then

placed a hand on his face. Her fingers were cool and soft. She must be able to feel the heat rolling off him. Heat she caused.

"Yes?" He held his body still, but the desire pulsed inside him. She had to come to him. If something made her frightened, and maybe he could guess at it, she had to be the driver now. He wouldn't be the reason she ran away.

"I want to kiss you."

"That's good because I want to kiss you too." He removed her hand from his cheek and kissed her palm. "But not just like that."

"How would you feel if it were just a kiss?"

"If you kissed me, I'd feel pretty damn good." He choked out a laugh and a small smile tugged at her lips.

"No, I mean what if we only kissed and nothing more? No touching. Would you be okay with that?"

"Whatever you want is fine by me." He would be the luckiest man in Hunterdon County if Brooklyn Wilde kissed him again.

"But we've already been together. I would understand if you expected more from me."

"Hey." He cupped her face so she could see how serious he was. "I would never expect anything from you. The past is the very long ago past, and we were different people. Tonight is like starting over. If all we did was hold each other, that would be fine with me."

Tears brimmed in her eyes. "I need to tell you something first."

"Whatever you need to do." Someone had hurt her, and if it was that ex-husband, he would punch him right in the face when he got here. He didn't want Brooklyn borrowing money from that guy, if he did anything to her.

"Last year, I was attacked. A man in a parking lot took everything, including my dignity. It's why I have the nightmares. It's why I'm afraid to be alone at night, and why I'm divorced. I don't know if I'm ready to have sex yet." She held his gaze, but her lip trembled.

He wanted to hurt whoever had done this to her. He would rip their throats out if he could, but violence wouldn't solve anything and wasn't what she needed. He pushed away the blinding rage and gathered her in his arms. "I'm sorry that happened to you. You didn't deserve it."

"It's changed who I am." Her palms splayed over his back, sending a potent current over his skin.

"No, it hasn't. You're still the same smart beautiful woman you always were." He kissed the top of her head. He would never hurt her. And that meant nothing could happen between them. She deserved a man who could care for her the right way. Someone who would stick around and be the rock she needed. He couldn't stay here. Not if Vetter was determined to throw him in jail.

"But now I'm afraid, and I don't know where I belong. At least not until I came home. And not until I found out Cordy wanted to sell the farm. This is where I belong."

In her arms sure seemed like where he belonged, but he couldn't say that. He wouldn't promise her anything he couldn't deliver on. "You'll get the farm. Your husband will lend you the money." He eased out of the embrace. Better to keep a distance between them or he was liable to kiss her.

She took her tea mug and rinsed it at the sink. "Ex-husband. He couldn't handle what happened to me. He stopped touching me. He wouldn't come near me or would cringe if I touched him. I guess that's also why I'm a little uncertain about being with a man. I worry every man will feel the way he does."

He stared at her back unsure of what to say. He still wanted to punch her ex. How could he treat Brooklyn as if she were damaged? Nothing that had happened had been her fault and he didn't have to know the whole story to know that. If she were his wife, he would have made sure she knew how beautiful and desirable she was. He would never take her for granted and always be the unmoving force in her life. He would be the lucky one.

"You don't have to worry, Brooklyn. Not every man feels the way he does." He certainly didn't. He wanted nothing more than to take her hand and lead her to the bedroom where he could show her all night how she turned him on.

"You just stopped touching me too." She went into the living room, and he followed. The room was dark except for the light filtering down the hall from the kitchen, and the glow of the moon coming through the window.

"Not because I don't want to."

"Then why?" She grabbed the blanket off the back of the sofa and wrapped it around her as if she wanted to protect herself from him.

"Because once I start, I won't be able to stop. And I don't mean I can't control myself. I meant what I said before. If all you want to do is kiss, then that's it. I mean once I start loving you, I won't be able to get enough. And I'm not the kind of man you need."

"It's funny how everyone—you, my father, brother and grandmother—seems to think they know what I need better than I do. I need a man who's willing to take his time with me. I'm not asking for a lifetime commitment from you."

"You deserve the kind of man that can stick around and make a life with you. I can't stay in Candlewood Falls. After what happened tonight, I should be on the road by daybreak. My presence here is only going to hurt you. I can't let that happen."

"Don't let those narrow-minded men run you out of the only home you've ever known."

"It's not my home anymore. And it's not just them. It's everyone who still believes I killed SJ. Your father. Your brother. Your uncle. Even Mrs. Holloway has me pegged for the man who broke into her home." The accusation would always hang over him. He'd never be free here. But she was right about this town being the only home he'd ever known. He had never felt the connection to any other place the way he did here. He came back every year to visit his mother, but also to smell the trees and the scent of apples in the air, and to drive down the streets he roamed as a kid.

"She hasn't said that. She isn't sure who broke into her home. The police have no evidence against you."

"They didn't last time either." This whole night weighed on him. The pain in his chest and stomach from the kicking ached. He dropped onto the sofa and wiped a hand over his face.

"You were leaning over SJ's body and covered in his blood. This time you weren't anywhere near Mrs. H's house." She sat beside him, and he wanted to sigh with relief just because she was close to him. When she was close, he could think.

"I was actually. I was out on the road. Only I was knocked out and no one saw me."

"I already told them you were with me."

"You lied." And he hadn't wanted her to.

"I helped." She gave a nod as if to emphasize the point.

"You could get in trouble. You don't want that kind of trouble." He would never forgive himself if she ended up in jail because of him. He wasn't worth it.

"Let me worry about that."

"Don't get tangled up with these men. Not after what you've been through. In the morning, I'll be on my way. If my bike isn't ready, I'll have Jameson send it to me."

"What if I don't want you to go?"

"Why would you want me to stay?" He was grateful for the darkness of the room. He couldn't bear to look her in the eye to find out she might be lying again. Why would she want him to stay? Because they had a history together? Or was it because she trusted him just enough to try and have sex with him. He was flattered, but he didn't want just sex.

"Because, when I'm with you I don't feel like a victim." Her words were hushed.

"We haven't been around each other that long. How can I do that for you?"

"You did it for me before. Don't you remember?"

Of course, he did. He had never forgotten.

CHAPTER ELEVEN

"Caleb, say something." Did he remember what he had done for her? She had never forgotten.

Brooklyn shifted on the sofa. She wanted to be closer to him, but she didn't want Caleb to push her away. She should have just kissed him and not told her story to him. But she had been worried she wouldn't have been able to perform. She hadn't wanted to start something she couldn't finish. And boy, had she wanted to start something.

"I remember that night, if that's what you're looking for me to say."

"You were the only person in school who hadn't made me feel as if what happened was my fault."

"It wasn't. That guy had acted like an asshole. I just put a stop to it."

It had been a Friday night after the football game her senior year. Probably around the same time of year it was now. There could be a chill in the air or warm enough to go to the game in a short-sleeved shirt. Football was a big deal in a town as small as Candlewood Falls. The team had won and everyone was celebrating who was still at the field. Her father was expecting her home, but she had lost track of time in all the fun.

The air had smelled like woodsmoke and the field had been littered with confetti. Someone from the marching band had left behind their trumpet on the bleachers. She could still see the brass twinkling from the field lights even after all these years.

Her friends had all left, believing she had everything under control. That was what she had believed too. But there had been a boy. Someone from the other school. Tall and muscular. More street-smart than she was with her small-town living. He had seemed nice enough, kept trying to make her laugh. He had asked for her number and said goodbye.

She walked to the parking lot alone. She should've known then something wasn't right. What respectable young man would have left her by herself at that time of night with no one around? Her car had been the only one in the lot by the time she got there. The wind had picked up and blew her hair in front of her face and sent an icy tremor down her spine. The lights on the football field had snapped off, throwing her into complete darkness.

"If it hadn't been for you, I wouldn't have made it to the car." She quivered under the blanket even in the safety of her grandmother's house. She had been young and foolish back then. But not last year. Last year, she had just been at the wrong place at the wrong time.

The boy she had been speaking with had come up behind her. At first, he had said something funny to get her attention —she couldn't remember what it was—then he tried to kiss her. She had refused him, and he had smacked her. She fell to the ground in a heap. He had wanted the keys to her car. Had said it was his birthday, and he deserved a car.

She tried to stand, wanting to run as far and as fast as her legs would carry her, but he had grabbed her and shoved her against the car hard enough to dent it. His hands had been everywhere on her as she struggled to make him stop.

Caleb reached over to her now, sitting beside him on the sofa, and pulled her close. She snuggled against him, avoiding the spot where he was hurt, and relished the definition of his muscles under his shirt. "I saw that guy grab you," he said.

"Lucky for me you were still at the school. Why were you still there? I have never asked you that in all these years."

"I saw you with him, talking by the concession stand. I didn't like the way he was looking at you. And I can tell you now, I was jealous. I know we were just friends at that point, but you were more than that to me. I stuck around to make sure you got home safely."

"You beat him up pretty good."

"He deserved it."

"But you got into a lot of trouble. You did that for me." The boy had come back to the school with his friends, looking for Caleb. Another fight broke out, but it was Caleb who had to pay the price. The other boys ran before they were caught.

"It was a long time ago. It doesn't matter now. Let's talk about something else."

"It matters to me. You were my hero." That had been the moment her feelings for him changed from friendship. But when he had gone to prison, she hadn't been as brave as he had been. She had allowed her family to convince her that she didn't belong with him. He had never held that against her, not if holding her now was any indication.

"The last thing I was or am is a hero. I was just doing what was necessary." He shifted and winced.

She eased out his embrace to be able to see his face in the moonlight streaming in the window. She ran a finger over his hairline. "You should get some rest." Especially if he was leaving in the morning.

"I'm resting just fine. Is that why you believed I didn't kill SJ? Because I fought that boy for you?"

"I knew you didn't kill my uncle because you aren't that kind of person. Yes, you had more than your share of fights, but you would never beat someone to death. I only wish they had found the person who had killed him." She pulled the blanket over both of them, unable to think of any other place she'd rather be. If he wasn't going to go back to bed, he might as well be comfortable out on the couch beside her, wrapped up in the warmth of the fleece.

"If he had landed an inch in the other direction, he would've ended up with only a concussion." He tugged the blanket up to his chin and closed his eyes.

"He was drinking himself to death. My family knew that." And they had tried to stop him; well, her father and her other uncles did, but SJ was too far gone and unable to turn himself around in time. Her family had never suspected someone would hit SJ hard enough to kill him. To them, by all rights SJ should be alive. Or if his life had ended it should have been him, sitting on his couch, alone, with an empty bottle of whiskey beside him.

"They still blame me." Caleb's eyes remained closed.

"They do. And I'm sorry about that. I could talk to my father—"

"Don't do that. There isn't anything you could say that would change his mind or your brother's. Let it go. The best thing for me to do is leave you and this town. No one will hurt you if I'm gone." He settled further into the cushions.

She should slip away and let him sleep. He was injured

and needed rest. Her desire to be with him was selfish, but she wanted to feel like a whole woman again if only for one night, one single moment where she wasn't broken. She wanted to remember the way breathless anticipation brought her to life.

Caleb made her feel that way, and not because they had been together in the past. Because in the here and now, she felt more like herself when he was around than she had in the past year. He had soothed her soul in the way she hungered after when no one else could.

She understood he wasn't promising her anything other than to be gone by morning. Maybe the absence of a commitment was exactly what she needed—no strings attached, no explanations. Just one night to be her old self or perhaps a better version of the new one.

"Can I ask you something?" she said with her heart stuck in her throat.

He opened one eye, and she laughed, easing some of the tension inside her and giving her the courage to go on. "Shoot," he said.

"Would you kiss me now?" Her words were barely audible, even to her. She stared at her hands, not wanting to see the possible rejection in his eyes.

He sat up and the blanket fell to his lap. He tilted her chin, giving her nothing else to look at except him and the smile on his face. "Are you sure?"

"I mean, only if you still want to, and if it won't cause you anymore pain after what you went through earlier—"

"Brooklyn, stop talking and kiss me." The smile was full of mischief, and her body glowed.

She leaned in, not wanting to wait another second and pressed her lips to his soft ones. He tangled his fingers in her hair again and kissed her back. Her heart raced ahead, but her mind pulled it back. *Don't rush; there's danger at the end.* She pushed away the thoughts threatening to upend her little plan. She wanted to do this, to taste Caleb and feel every part of him. She put a hand behind his neck to increase the connection between them.

His hand traveled down her arm, leaving a line of delicious heat in its wake. If his simple touch could set her skin on fire, what would her body do when he reached her most intimate places? She shivered and inched closer, allowing her hands to explore the parts of his chest that weren't hurt.

His lips moved to her jaw, then down her neck. Her head hung back, giving him more space to kiss and play with his tongue. A moan escaped her lips.

"Nice," he said against her skin. His fingers rubbed lightly across the scar on the other side of her neck.

She hesitated, but scolded herself. She was safe with Caleb. He was the boy who had saved her. She had fallen for him once. Her heart was falling again. Of that she was certain. The mind, though, could play terrible tricks, could convince of anything, even a non-truth.

He eased away from her and held her gaze. "Are you sure you're okay with this?"

She ran a finger over the scruff on his strong jaw. "You're beautiful, you know that?" The bruising and cuts took nothing away from his good looks.

He ducked his head. "Not the word I'd use. You are the beautiful one. More beautiful now, but please tell me if you want to stop. You can be honest with me."

"I want to be with you. Don't think that I don't."

He brushed the hair away from her face and looked at her with a bittersweetness, as if he understood what she wasn't saying. She still needed some time. Not because she didn't trust him. She didn't trust herself.

"When you're ready, I will be there, if you still want me

to." He kissed her cheek, then struggled to push off the couch.

He limped away.

And she let him go.

∾

Brooklyn sat up with a jolt. Her neck screamed in protest. She had fallen asleep on the sofa after Caleb went to bed. The sun had barely snuck into the sky, leaving the room in early-morning muted grays. Lucy screeched her warning sounds. Some of the other alpacas had joined her in making an orchestra of noise.

She jumped off the couch and grabbed a coat to throw over her t-shirt. Something was wrong. The shotgun was upstairs in the closet. She turned toward the stairs, but changed course and ran for the door. She hoped she wasn't making a mistake.

The alpacas' feeder had been turned over, and hay spilled all over the ground and into the mud puddle in the grass. Lucy and Ethel ran in circles on their side of the barn, screeching as they went and bouncing into one another like furry bumper cars. The boys huddled in the corner of theirs. The barn had been trashed. Tools were scattered and broken. Garbage was thrown everywhere. The barn floor was covered in what was most likely manure. She clasped a hand over her mouth to keep back the bile.

Even the fence Caleb had just repaired had been torn down. A yellow piece of paper was nailed to the tree. She hesitated to grab it, in case it might burn her.

Holding her breath, she tore the paper from the nail.

We'll do worse if you let that murderer stay.

The screen door slapped against the house. She turned to find Caleb on the porch, staring wide-eyed and still wearing the clothes he had slept in. "What the hell happened? Are the alpacas hurt?"

"They're just upset." As was she and rightfully so. She held out the note. He marched over in two strides and snatched it. His gaze ran over the paper. A scowl distorted his face.

"They have no right to do this to you. Someone has to pay. I'll make them pay." He crushed the paper in his fist.

No matter what she thought about Caleb, or the way her body responded to him, she couldn't deny he was the reason this was all unfolding. Someone had broken into Mrs. Holloway's house, stolen from her, and terrorized her. Caleb had been in nothing but fights since he arrived. And now her grandmother's life's work was in jeopardy. Was he really who she thought he was?

"I want to stay here and fight whoever is doing this to you. They can push me around, but they can't do it to you. I won't let them. Tell me to stay, Brooklyn. I will. I will make sure whoever did this to you, never does it again. I promise that. Tell me. Tell me what you want me to do." His fist shook.

She stared at him and then the barn. Her alpacas could have been hurt. She wouldn't be able to live with herself if something happened to those sweet creatures. She wanted this farm more than she had wanted anything in a long time. She was even willing to deal with Oliver in order to have it, and he would be there later in the morning. She owed Caleb nothing. They had been in each other's company only a few short days. It would be better for everyone if he left town today and never returned. She could go back to her peaceful little life she'd created here, and hope to convince Cordy to sell her the farm and not Brad. Didn't she want to stay hidden? Wasn't that why she had run home six months ago?

"Brooklyn, answer me. Tell me what you want me to do." His words snapped her out of her runaway thoughts.

She took in his handsome face and the pain in his eyes. What had happened on this farm had happened to him too. He was as much of a victim as she was.

"Stay."

CHAPTER TWELVE

Brooklyn stood at the window in the living room and looked out. Oliver's silver Lexus bounced down the unpaved driveway, sending clouds of dirt into the air. He would be cursing under his breath about the dust and the knicks to his paint job. She took a long steadying breath. He wasn't her problem any longer. She only needed his money.

She saw no point in waiting for him to come to the door. She met him at the car before he could even get out. The weather had held, which was to her advantage. Rain or a damp wind would only make him impatient with walking around a muddy farm. He almost never came to Candlewood Falls with her in all the years they had been together. He couldn't understand her father's need to live off the grid or her grandmother's obsession with alpacas. Even the orchard was too farm-like for him.

"I forgot what a long drive it is out here. We really are in the middle of nothing. Isn't it too quiet for you?" Oliver stretched his back and rolled his head on his neck.

"I love the quiet. In fact, it could be quieter." She would keep a positive attitude no matter what he said to her. But she did find peace in the open space and the tall trees in the distance. Noise and too many people in one area still made her nerves fray.

"I can't figure out why you prefer to be out here with no shopping, no culture, not even a real highway in a seven-mile radius."

"Candlewood Falls has all that. And anything it doesn't have I can get to in an hour. This is the best place to live. Come on, let me show you around." She waved him over, ready to end the conversation about Candlewood Falls' location. He would never see this place the way she did. That was fine with her. She certainly didn't want him deciding to buy a house out here.

He placed a cold, wet kiss too close to her lips. What had she ever seen in him? He was attractive with his dimpled smile and hazel eyes. He worked out and stayed in shape, but inside he was one-dimensional, empty.

She led him to the alpacas. Caleb had done a great job of cleaning up. Other than her missing tools, she could barely tell someone had vandalized the barn. Lucy screeched at Oliver, then hurried away. Ethel eyed him from her corner. Alistair pranced over, his neck bobbing back and forth, to check Oliver out. Oliver jumped out of the way, waving his arms in the air.

She stifled a laugh. "He won't hurt you. He just wants to say hello."

"Do they bite?" His face scrunched up in disgust.

"Of course not. They are gentle giants. They make great pets even if someone doesn't want to use their fleece or breed them. They're less maintenance than dogs. Isn't that right, Alistair?" She ran her fingers through his soft fleece at the top of his head. In the spring, they would be sheared and only the tops of their heads would keep the fluffy stuff, giving them that puffy head look alpacas get.

"I think I'll stick with a fish. Who's the guy fixing the fence?"

"That's Caleb. He's helping out around here for a few weeks." She grabbed Oliver's elbow and directed him toward the gift store and away from Caleb.

He asked her questions about how much profit the store made, and if she had plans to expand it. He wanted to know her five-year business plan, and how long she planned to take to pay him back.

"I want to add weddings to the list of services we provide. Rustic weddings are very popular and not too many places offer them." She went on to explain more about her vision. He only asked questions, but never criticized. She tried not to get her hopes up too much. Oliver could just as easily bark out that her ideas were a waste of time.

"Sounds like you thought this all through." He turned, taking in the farm again, and hesitating on Caleb at the fence. He reached for her and took her hand. "Brooklyn, I know I wasn't the best husband to you always. I can see you're getting your life together here, even if I think you're making a mistake by leaving nursing for a bunch of furry, weird-looking animals."

He was going to tell her no by saying something nice first. Typical Oliver. She pulled her hand away. "Nursing doesn't fit me anymore. I need and want a change. This farm is the path I've been looking for."

"You've needed a lot of changes recently. After we split, I didn't think you'd move away. Didn't you have a nice life in Montclair?"

"Is this your way of telling me no?" She wasn't going to answer his question. Her life there had been wrapped up in his. Once they split, she had nothing. Her friends were the women married to the men he associated with. Those women didn't want to be friends with her afterward. Her job had no longer fulfilled her. And the town was too crowded. Everywhere she turned, she feared someone would come up behind her.

"Is that what you think I was going to say?"

"Isn't it? Just say it. You don't see the alpaca farm as a good investment." Might as well get the worst over with.

He shook his head. "I'll lend you the money. I want you to be happy. I really do."

As she opened her mouth to thank him, a small red car sped down the driveway, bouncing on the uneven spots as if it might take flight. She didn't recognize the car or the driver, but could tell it was a woman with blond hair. No one she knew. Caleb joined them then. Sweat glistened on his face and arms. Dirt covered his strong hands and corded forearms from all the work he'd been doing. A ripple of excitement ran over her skin. Dirt looked good on him, and she'd like the chance to clean him up.

"Who's that?" Caleb said, interrupting her sexual thoughts about him. Heat climbed up her neck, probably leaving big red splotches that gave her away.

Oliver's head turned with a snap. "Looks like she has a guest. Oliver Moore." He stuck out his hand. "And you are?"

"Caleb Ransom." He wiped his hand on his jeans before shaking.

"Have we met? You seem familiar."

"Nope."

They hadn't ever met. Oliver had heard Caleb's name throughout the years from stories her family told, not all good. She wasn't going to remind him of that. The car careening down the drive came to a halt, and the back door swung open.

Cordy threw her hands in the air. Bracelets in a rainbow of colors slid down her thin arms. Her smile electrified her beautiful and wise face. The breeze caught her long white hair and lifted it off her shoulders. "I'm home, and it looks like the party already started without me." She dragged her suitcase out of the backseat, patted the driver on the shoulder, and sashayed over to them.

"Welcome back." She gripped her grandmother in a tight hug and inhaled the comforting smell of lavender that always surrounded Cordy. "I've missed you. You're back a day early." She hadn't expected to see Cordy until Oliver was long gone and didn't want to explain his appearance at the farm. Not after all the things she had shared with Cordy about her marriage and it's unraveling.

"I missed you too. I have so much to tell you, but first, what's with the men?" Cordy continued the embrace and whispered in her ear.

"I'll tell you everything soon." She squeezed Cordy's shoulders.

"Hello, Cordy. It's very nice to see you again." Oliver stepped forward with his hand stretched out.

"Oliver. Hello. I didn't expect to see you here. I hope you're making yourself useful." She turned away from Oliver, leaving his hand in midair. "Caleb, my dear boy, come give me a hug. It has been way too long since I saw you last." She held up her outstretched arms.

Oliver snorted. Caleb did as he was told, but didn't linger in the embrace. "I don't want to get you dirty," he said.

"A little dirt never hurt anyone. How's that motorcycle? Has Jameson fixed it yet?" Cordy adjusted her bracelets.

"No, ma'am. Still waiting. Thank you for the room in the meantime."

She waved a hand in the air. "Stop ma'aming me. You're like family. If you're helping out around here, then you've more than paid your keep. Brooklyn told me about your accident." She gripped his chin with two fingers and examined his fading bruises and scars. "Looks like you lost to the road. Did you see Doc?"

"Not this time. I'm healing up fine. I'm going to clean up. If you'll excuse me." He nodded and hurried off without another word.

"How are my babies?" Cordy took in the barn but didn't seem to notice anything out of place. She would have to tell her about the vandalism, but after Oliver left.

"Everyone is behaving," she said. "Why don't we go inside, and you can tell us all about the trip."

"Um," Oliver said, scratching the back of his neck. "I'm going to make my way to the hotel over in the next town, out on the highway. I'll be here until tomorrow. Brooklyn, call me tonight so we can finalize your details."

"What details are those?" Cordy said, moving her gaze between her and Oliver.

"Okay, great. I'll call you. Thanks for coming out." She didn't want one of the guys to tell Cordy before she could. She wanted to have the conversation in person about buying the farm instead of Brad, just Cordy and her.

"Take care, Cordy." Oliver stretched out his hand, but pulled it back as if he thought better of trying to shake again.

"Same to you, Oliver." Cordy stood statue straight. Brooklyn tried not to laugh. Cordy let everyone know where they stood with her. She loved that about her grandmother.

They watched as Oliver turned his car around and drove back to the road, both of them silent. The wind had picked up and whisked away the blue sky, replacing it with pregnant rain clouds. A chill clung to the air, desperate to claim the afternoon in her cold grip. Brooklyn pulled her sweater closed. The weather could change without warning in the fall just the way life could.

"Okay, what gives? Why was Oliver here, and what is he talking about?" Cordy's intense gaze met hers.

"Don't you want to get settled from your trip first? Are you hungry?" She offered a lame attempt to avoid the conversation. She had thought she'd have another day to prepare her speech.

"Don't manage me, Brooklyn. Your ex-husband was here for a reason. Are you thinking about going back to him?" Cordy dug a fleece cardigan out of her travel bag and shoved her arms in it.

"What? Reconnect with Oliver? Absolutely not. Never. I needed a favor. That's all. It's cold out here. Let's go inside."

Cordy fisted her hand on a hitched hip. "You won't blow away in the wind. Spill it."

"Fine. I didn't want to tell you standing in the driveway, but here goes." She took a deep breath. "I want you to sell the farm to me instead of Brad."

"You want the farm? Why?"

That wasn't the answer she expected. Of all the people in the world, Cordy understood her the best. She always seemed to know what she needed before she did. She had come to rely on Cordy's intuition or good sense or whatever it was called. For her grandmother not to have seen what the farm and the animals had come to mean to her in the past six months poked a small hole in her heart the minute Cordy had announced her desire to sell.

"I love it here. This place has felt like home in a way nowhere else has. I thought you knew that."

Cordy grabbed her suitcase. "Let's go inside. You're right. It's cold out here. This conversation would be better had around the kitchen table with a hot cup of tea."

Inside, Cordy threw some logs on for a fire in the living room while Brooklyn put up the water for tea. The extra minutes gave her a chance to catch her breath. She would get right to the point and didn't see any reason to drag out the conversation. Prolonging their talk wouldn't take the sting away if Cordy insisted on selling the farm to Brad.

"We can have our tea in the living room. It will be warmer in there in a few minutes." Cordy washed her hands at the kitchen sink.

"Why don't you want me to have the farm?" She leaned against the counter, facing Cordy.

"Do we have any of my cheesecakes or loaves still in the freezer? I could go for a little pound cake." Cordy ignored her and went into the basement. It appeared they both were having some trouble getting this conversation off the ground.

She checked the farm's Instagram account for any comments that might need addressing as an excuse to stay busy while her grandmother went to the basement in search of dessert. Dessert that Brooklyn didn't need or want at the moment. She took a quick peek down the hall. Caleb's door was shut. Maybe he had heard their voices and was giving them some space.

Cordy returned holding a round cake wrapped in aluminum foil. "We're in luck. I can have this defrosted in fifteen minutes. Did you know you shouldn't defrost a pound cake in the refrigerator? It sucks out all the moisture." Cordy held the cake over her head as if she had won a trophy. She unwrapped the aluminum foil and the wax paper underneath before sliding the cake onto a foil-lined baking sheet and putting it in the cold oven. "It stays in until the oven heats up to two hundred fifty degrees. We want it warm. Not twice baked."

"Cordy, I don't want any cake." Or a lesson on baking. "I deserve an answer about the farm. I thought you'd be all for me buying it from you. I would keep the alpacas and the store. Brad is going to take everything down and do away with the animals to plant apple trees for the orchard." Trees they really didn't need, but Brad had big plans for the orchard that included a major expansion.

Cordy took the seat opposite her and clasped her age-spotted hand over hers. "I know that's what he wants. What I don't understand is why you want the farm. This wasn't your dream, sweety. You came back to heal. I understood that, but I assumed you'd move on again. You're like me that way, always moving, not sitting still. Like your mother too, I'm sorry to say because she's my daughter, and I love her, but that unsettled streak had her running away."

"I was running away when I came back here. I didn't know how to handle my life, but now I'm done running. I want to stay put in the one place that has the power to ground me." She tried to keep the frustration out of her voice, but failed. Six months ago, when she had returned with a few suitcases and a wounded soul, owning the alpaca farm had not been what she desired. She didn't know what she wanted then except some time to herself, time to lick her wounds without judgment from anyone.

Each day she had forced herself out of bed in the upstairs guest room of Cordy's farmhouse and fed the alpacas breakfast, all five loving her in spite of the hollowness inside. Ethel would nudge her with her head, wanting Brooklyn to pet her. Alpacino would gallop over and push his brothers out of the way for all the attention—from her. Alistair brought his rake as a gift. Chewpaca and Lucy would wait their turns for Brooklyn to notice them. The alpacas and their playfulness returned joy to her heart a tiny piece at a time.

She had survived the pain of what had happened to her in the routine of the farm and its beauty. The rolling hills welcomed her every day. They were her constant. Cordy's wind chimes played music for her in the damp spring, then hot summer, now crisp fall breeze. She had taken long walks around the property, letting the sun kiss her skin and the earth anchor her again. Now, it seemed as if Cordy hadn't noticed at all.

She had learned so much about the farm and herself. She would figure out the knitting part in time, and until then she would have to ship the yarn out for garments to be made. "Is this because he's a man?"

Cordy sat back in her seat and wiped the air clean with her hand. "Oh, pooh. A man. You know better than that. I've been running this farm for ages. Where was your grandfather? I loved that man with my heart and soul, but Levon didn't know the first thing about farm life except where to turn his car into the driveway."

"Then why do you think this place wouldn't be good for me?" Unwanted and unexpected tears burned her eyes. She blinked them away. She had no other plans for her future. If this farm went to Brad, where would she go?

The tea kettle burst into song loud enough to startle some of her emotions away. Grateful for something to do, she clambered out of the chair and prepared the tea.

"You didn't seem to take to the farm before this trip. You hardly visited after you moved away. I thought this time you were just trying to earn your keep. I didn't know you were falling in love with the place. I figured you had more of your mother in you than you realized, that's all. It's not bad. It's just a life here or similar to the one your father built isn't for everyone. Brad is better suited for farm life. He loves that orchard. Its dirt is in his blood."

"Are you saying, then, that you won't sell it to me?" Her throat closed in around her words. She swallowed hard, reprimanding herself for acting like a child who couldn't have her way. Disappointment was everywhere. She would have to make do if the farm went to Brad. But wasn't she entitled to a little luck thrown her way after the year she'd had?

"I think if I do sell it to you, you'll come in time to hate this place. You'll think you let me down or disappointed me because we don't have the same desires. If those alpacas will end up needing a home, I'd rather relocate them now and not worry about it."

"I belong here, Grandmother." She used that salutation because Cordy always hated being called any version of grandmother, and she wanted to drive her point home. "I belong here because of you. Because you made this a secure place for me. And not just now, but my whole life. I came home to you six months ago. I want to keep my home. How can you take it away from me?"

She stared her grandmother down, waiting for an answer. The tension in the space would snap in half if someone didn't speak.

"She's right, Cordy." Caleb's deep voice resonated from the doorway, vibrating in her chest. "This farm should go to Brooklyn. She belongs here. Don't be a fool and sell it to Brad."

CHAPTER THIRTEEN

Heat ran up Brooklyn's neck and burned her cheeks. Caleb may have gone too far with his last comment to Cordy, but she appreciated it all the same. Nobody seemed to understand her anymore except for Caleb. She would never have guessed he would be the one. She had often wondered if he was okay wherever life had taken him, but she never expected to find him inserted directly in the center of her life. She was glad he was.

"I overheard some of the conversation," he said. "Brooklyn sounded upset. I don't want her to lose her home. Brad can get land from somewhere else."

She mouthed a thank you so Cordy wouldn't see. He tipped his head in a small nod.

"What's going on between you two?" Cordy pushed away from the table and grabbed three mugs from the shelves.

"We're friends." She avoided Caleb's gaze. They were more than friends, but she didn't know how much more or if he wanted more, and she didn't want to explain any of it to Cordy.

Cordy placed a mug in front of her and one at the open

spot at the table. She pointed to Caleb and directed him to sit. He pulled out the chair without a word but kept his hands in his lap.

He had taken a shower. The ends of his hair were still wet and had left water spots on the collar of his shirt. His soapy smell mingled with the herbs coming from the tea. She wondered if his skin was still warm from the water and what it would taste like if she ran her tongue over it. Okay, clearly, she needed to pull herself together.

Cordy returned to her perch by the counter. "Let me get this straight. You show up in the middle of the night, and my nurse granddaughter comes to your aid. She opens her house to you, which you accept, and you watch her with eyes like a hawk. You don't let her out of your sight when you're present. I saw the way you eyed Oliver out there. Can't say I blame you. Not a fan either. Can you argue with any of that so far?"

"No, ma—"

Cordy held up a hand.

"Sorry. No, I'm not arguing. I owe Brooklyn a lot. I don't want anything to happen to her. She belongs on this farm."

"Hello, I'm sitting right here." She waved her hands in the air.

Caleb turned to her. "I'm sorry. I'm not trying to speak for you. I want to help you. You deserve to be happy, and this might not make me popular, but Brad doesn't deserve this farm. He doesn't need this farm."

She forced her face to stay neutral. She didn't want to give away to him or Cordy how much his words affected her. This man, so unexpected, dropped on her doorstep, almost literally, and became her biggest advocate as if he'd been standing by her side for years. When he had gone off to prison, the pain he felt and the pain her family had felt had been too much for her to handle at the time. She had walked away from him without much of an explanation, had left him to deal with his new circumstances alone and most certainly afraid. Now he sat in her kitchen fighting for her dreams.

"Do you love her?" Cordy said. "Because you sound like you're in love, young man."

Caleb remained silent, which deafened her as much as a tolling bell in a watch tower. She couldn't stay another second in that kitchen with its cheery walls and open shelves, waiting for him to say no. Not when it became painfully obvious to her that she could very well be in love with him.

She pushed out of the chair hard enough to knock it over, and she ran from the house, her lungs begging not to work. The screen door slapped closed behind her, punctuating the end of her embarrassment. Her heart could not take another piece broken off.

"Brooklyn, wait," Caleb called after her. His heavy footsteps pounded the dirt, gaining on her.

She ran past the fence he had fixed earlier and into the field. If she kept going, she would run into the orchard and the river that separated her family's business with the old winery owned by crazy Weezer River.

He caught up to her and grabbed her arm. "Wait," he said in between heavy breaths.

She stopped but pulled her arm away. Her chest heaved from the thwarted escape. "I want to be alone."

Cordy had done the unthinkable by bringing up any mention of love. Caleb couldn't possibly be in love with her. The idea that she could love him so quickly without his obvious return of feelings was what had sent her running like a loon.

"What Cordy said—"

"Drop it." She couldn't allow him to continue and embarrass them both. "She likes to play matchmaker. She's worse than my grandfather Skip. Two old coots always meddling in other people's lives. I was more upset about losing the farm, and then I guess I was embarrassed that she put you on the spot like that. I'm sorry. She shouldn't have done that."

"Can I speak now?"

She braced herself for whatever he might throw at her and hoped she wouldn't regret letting him talk. "Yes. Go ahead."

"You won't interrupt me?" He arched a brow, and his top lip curled up in a mirthful smile.

"The stage is all yours." Dragging this conversation out only made the humiliation worse. She should just let him have his say and be done with it. Like ripping duct tape off of hairy skin.

He stepped closer and laced his fingers through hers. She stared at their joined hands while her breathing returned to normal. Being with him seemed like the most natural thing. Some of the tightness in her chest eased.

"If someone had told me two weeks ago I would be standing in a field holding Brooklyn Wilde's hands, I would've had myself a good laugh. And not because I didn't want to hold your hands. But because I don't have that kind of luck. When that car cut me off the other night, and I crashed, the last thing I remembered thinking before I blacked out was figures, it's just my fucking luck."

"You're luckier than you realize. You could've died that night." And how horrible that would've been.

"Yeah, well, you might be right. My luck definitely changed some that night. I woke up in the ditch, covered in blood and soaked through from the rain. When I got to my feet, I realized exactly where I was and knew I could get some help. If I had fallen anywhere other than Cordy's farm, I would've limped me and my bike to the town line, and I would've missed seeing you."

"I'm glad you didn't." She squeezed his hand. She had been so scared when the pounding on the door had woken her. She thought for sure she would have to shoot someone because she would never again allow someone to hurt her. When she saw it was Caleb, relief had nearly knocked her to her knees. But his appearance had become more than just a familiar face at the door. She never imagined she would be drawn to him the way a flower stretched to reach the warmth of the sun.

"I don't believe in fate or destiny. I believe in what I can touch and what I can see. I don't think with my heart or any of that stuff printed on cards." He shrugged.

He was going to give her the *let's be friends* speech. She pulled her hand free from his.

A darkness passed over his brown eyes. "I don't think I'm saying this right."

"I get it. You just want to be friends. Cordy read into what's going on between us, and you want to clear the air. You like me just fine as a friend, but that's it."

He ran a hand over his face. "Wow, I really did screw that up, if that's what you think I meant."

"That's not what you're saying?"

"How about if I try this?" He cupped her face and brought his lips to hers.

She leaned into the kiss without hesitation and gripped his arms. He slid his hands down her back and brought her against his chest. She wrapped her arms around his neck and wanted more. So much more.

She opened her mouth to take the kiss deeper, and her body woke up. Her soul had been muted like a gray day, but with Caleb holding her and kissing her like no other man had ever, her body became a symphony of colors swirling inside her, bursting to be set free.

He eased out of the kiss, moving his lips closer to her ear.

"Am I making sense now?" His words were hot against her skin, a delicious heat that made her shiver.

"Perfect sense." She closed her eyes and relished the definition of his hard body next to hers. Without much convincing, she would lie down in the grass with him and strip him of his clothes.

He met her gaze, never putting more than an inch between them. His hands still rested against her back. "I want to do that again and again. And when you're ready, I want to do more. Is that okay with you?"

"But you're going to leave town."

"Would you let me stay?"

"But what about Vetter and the guys that are after you?"

"I'll figure something out. I don't know what yet, but I'll think of something, if you'll have me. I know I'm not much of a prize. I don't even have a job at the moment, but I promise I'll keep you safe."

"I want to keep you safe too. I won't stand for anyone pushing you around."

He choked out a laugh. "I know you will. You're one tough lady." He took her hand and turned in the direction they came from. "What are you going to do about the farm?"

"Convince Cordy to sell it to me somehow." She had no idea how, but she would think of something too. "We'll get to the bottom of our problems together."

"I don't want you trying to run interference with Vetter or any of the men from the Watchmen group. Let me handle them," he said.

"I can help with that."

"Brooklyn, please let me do it. I know you can handle yourself, but if anything ever happened to you, I wouldn't be able to forgive myself. Those men won't care if they hurt you. In fact, they'll enjoy doing it. They only pretend to be law-abiding citizens. Being with me is going to bring you plenty of trouble."

She would have a word with her father. Maybe he could talk to Huck and make him keep his men away from Caleb. Caleb wasn't bothering anyone, and she cared for him. Huck would listen to her dad. He was the only brother Huck respected enough to take advice from. Huck admired her father's decision to separate from society. But the difference between the men was Silas wasn't a criminal nor would he be. Huck thought anarchy against society was the answer. And he wanted an army of men who looked and thought just like him. Sometimes she was amazed how Huck could be from the same parents as his four brothers who were so different than he was.

They passed the fence. The alpacas came out to greet them. Alistair brought Caleb the rake again and dropped it at his feet.

"He likes playing that game with you." Her heart warmed at the scene of the animals and Caleb. She really had found her home.

Cordy watched from the screen door, the mug of tea still in her hand. Even from this distance, the smugness on Cordy's face was unmistakable. She must believe she had called what she saw between her and Caleb. Maybe it was love, maybe not. If they were given the time, she'd like to find out.

Now the next question became, if she found her home, here with Caleb, how was she going to keep it?

~

"I'm going to sleep in the gift shop," Caleb said. He had thought long and hard about that. Brooklyn and her grandmother needed their space to work through their differences.

His presence wasn't going to allow that to happen. He had considered finding somewhere else to stay altogether, but he didn't want to be too far from Brooklyn. Not after the threats made on him and in turn, her.

"That's ridiculous." She blocked his path to the front door and crossed her arms over her chest. He could lift her right off her feet and plop her off to the side, but he refrained. Her tilted chin and defiant stare ran all his heat south and made his limbs tingle.

The other reason he wanted to sleep in the gift shop was to be respectable to Cordy. Now that she was home, and he and Brooklyn wanted to take their relationship further, sleeping somewhere else seemed more appropriate. It didn't matter that they were all grown-ups. He still saw Cordy as a grandmother figure too.

"I think it looks better if I'm not sleeping here." He lowered his voice and ran a thumb over her jaw. Her soft skin was in contrast to his rough and calloused touch. Everything about them was opposite, and yet she still fit with him.

"You've already been sleeping here. What's changed? My grandmother is home? She knows what goes on between couples, and we haven't even done that yet." She lowered her voice too.

"I'm not doing that with her here. It's not right." He wanted to make love to Brooklyn more than anything else, but under her grandmother's roof wasn't going to cut it. He'd feel like a teenager again, listening for when the parents came home. He wanted to make their first time special for her. She deserved that after what she'd been through.

"I appreciate the chivalry, but you don't have to sleep in the shop. It's cold and uncomfortable. You can stay in your room. I won't even come downstairs until the sun is up, if that makes you feel better."

"Let me do this. I want to prove to your grandmother I'm

worthy of you. I'll just be on the other side of the yard. Text me if you need me, and I'll run right back."

She snaked her arms around his waist and tugged him close. "Let's get something straight. There's nothing wrong with you and me together. We've just started trying each other out. She would never deny us some happiness. Don't you think we both deserve it?" She stood on her toes and kissed him.

Thoughts of sleeping went right out of his head as she opened her mouth to him. She tasted minty, and his head spun. He wanted to scoop her up and carry her off to the bedroom where he could show her all night long how he felt about her. Words were not his thing. He didn't know how to express his emotions that way. He had pushed all his emotions down so far, he could barely touch them. Anger was the only thing he knew how to feel, but with this woman, she made him want to swim in the current of warmth and security. Her smell and her touch brought him home, and he hadn't had a home in over twelve years.

Her hands ran over his back and slid inside the back pockets of his jeans, grabbing his ass. She pressed against him, making him want to remove their clothing so nothing was between them. He dared to reach under her shirt and place his palm on the flat of her belly. If she pushed him away, he wouldn't hesitate, but when she didn't, he moaned.

"Don't mind me. Just getting some tea." Cordy's cackle of a laugh tore them apart.

Heat ran back up his torso and burned his face. That was exactly what he didn't want to happen. He could only hope Cordy hadn't heard any of the sounds they had made.

Brooklyn tried to wipe her mouth with the back of her hand. "I was just telling Caleb he didn't need to sleep in the gift shop. You don't mind if he stays in the guest room downstairs, do you?" She placed a hand on his arm and leaned into him. He kind of needed her to stand in front of him, but he didn't dare move. He wasn't even sure if he could speak at the moment.

"It's warmer with the alpacas. If you're nice, Alpacino will cuddle with you." Cordy kept a straight face for two beats before winking and slapping her leg with a good laugh.

He needed to sit down because suddenly he wanted to vomit.

Cordy shook her head. "Caleb, the color has drained clean away from your face. You young people don't know how to take a joke. You can sleep in Brooklyn's room, if you want. I'm pretty sure you already took her virginity away."

"Cordy." Brooklyn screeched like Lucy the alpaca.

Cordy waved her hand in the air. "Like I didn't know that. I'm glad to see you two finally giving it another try. You're way better for her than Oliver. Sorry. Saying it as I see it." Cordy went about making her tea, ignoring both of them.

He turned to Brooklyn. "I'll sleep in my room." He needed her to understand he meant business. He needed to hang on to some dignity.

"Fine."

From the set of her jaw, he wasn't sure it was fine at all, but it would have to be. He would behave like a gentleman and take a cold shower. He kissed her on the cheek. "Good night. Good night, Cordy."

"Night." She waved over her head.

He stole one final glance at Brooklyn before he slipped down the hall. He smiled, hoping she would smile back. Instead, she tilted that chin and marched away. He didn't understand women at all. He closed the door to his room and raked his hands over his face. Sleep would not come tonight. And neither would he.

CHAPTER FOURTEEN

Brooklyn stood outside Caleb's room and took a steadying breath. She couldn't sleep, knowing he was downstairs alone. She appreciated what he was trying to do for her grandmother, but she was ready to spend the night with him. She wanted to take advantage of her recent burst of courage in case it dried up. She suspected having sex with him would be wonderful, but suspecting wasn't enough. She had to know. Just that thought surprised her because she had been certain not that long ago that she may never want to have sex again. She shouldn't be shocked. Caleb had given her a peacefulness in a way no one had before. He was thoughtful and caring. He loved the alpacas as much as she did and wanted to see her dreams come true.

She knocked and hoped he didn't turn her away.

The door opened. He blinked, raising an arm to lean against the door and flexing the muscles of his bare torso. His hair was messed, making him look sexier, if that was even possible.

Her gaze followed the line of chest hair that tapered below his navel and ran under the band of his sweatpants.

Her fingers reached for her scar. She forced them back to her side.

"Is everything okay?" Sleepiness rattled around in his deep voice.

"I couldn't sleep. I was wondering if I could lie with you and see if that helps."

He held the door wider and allowed her to pass. She ducked under his arm, catching a whiff of his soapy smell. Her heart picked up speed. Sneaking in here made her feel as if she were getting away with something.

The room was dark except for the moonlight streaming in. He hadn't closed the shades. This room faced the pasture, and even if it faced the road, no one could see the house from there. Her eyes adjusted, allowing her to make out the shadow of the bed and the rocking chair with his clothes strewn across it.

"Which side of the bed do you want?" He remained by the door.

"I don't care." But she did want him to come closer to her. Maybe meet her halfway so she wouldn't feel like a complete fool coming onto him in the middle of the night after he had made it clear he didn't want to have sex while Cordy slept only feet away.

"Why can't you sleep? Did you have another nightmare?" He still didn't move.

"Not this time. I was thinking about you. About the farm, I guess. I thought I might feel more relaxed with your arms around me." That was the truth, but she wanted some other things to happen before the sleeping part.

He walked past her but didn't touch her. She tugged on the end of the nightshirt she had worn and wondered if she should've come down in something sexier. Like nothing.

He held up the blankets. "You can have the right. I'll take the other side."

She slipped under the covers. The sheets were cool against her bare legs. He covered her and went around the bed. He slid in beside her, his heat instantly warming her. The bed was a full size, not giving them a lot of extra room which she was grateful for. If this were a king size bed, it would be too easy for him to slip away. He draped an arm over her shoulder and pulled her close. She snuggled against him, discovering the quick rhythm of his heart. She wondered if he was feeling any of the nerves she was.

"Thank you for letting me sleep over." She tried to make a joke, but he didn't laugh. She second-guessed her decision to come downstairs. He certainly had seemed interested in taking things further when he kissed her in front of the door earlier. Maybe he really couldn't be persuaded to break his own rule.

"We're just sleeping," he said.

Damn his moral compass. She wasn't sure if sleep would be any easier lying next to him while he was half-dressed. Her fingers wanted to disobey and explore the hills and valleys of his body.

She pushed up to get a better look at his face. She was pretty sure his jaw covered in day-old beard was locked in a tight line. She wanted to touch that too.

"Caleb, I don't want to just sleep."

He threw back the covers and jumped out of the bed. "You aren't making this easy on me."

"I don't understand. We both want this, or am I wrong?" She wasn't trying to force him. That would not be right, but she wanted him, and she was pretty sure if they were anywhere else, this wouldn't even be a discussion.

"I want you. This. Us. But ever since I left prison, I try to live my life by doing the right thing. I don't ever want to give anyone a reason to believe the worst of me because once they find out I was in jail, even though I was exonerated, they still act like I'm garbage. Making love to you in Cordy's house is wrong. Call me old-fashioned." He ran a hand through his hair, making it messier and sexier.

She climbed out of bed and went to him. She wanted to touch him, but hesitated. "You are a man of honor. I admire the creed you live your life by. We are two consenting adults and this is my house too. I'm a grown woman who is divorced and has had some bad things happen in her life. Ever since my attack, I promised myself I would be truthful about what I wanted. I didn't want to deny myself happiness anymore. I want you, Caleb. In my house. Tonight. If you don't want me too, then I'll go, but if you do, then please make love to me."

He didn't say anything. She held her breath, waiting for an answer because if he didn't say he wanted to make love too, she would have to leave and go back to her room. Where she would hide from eternal embarrassment.

"Don't go." He pulled her to him. "I wanted our first time to be special. Somewhere romantic. You deserve that."

She wrapped her arms around his neck. "This is special because I want you. I want you to touch me. You are the man that made that possible for me. You reminded me how to feel again."

He lifted her off her feet as if she weighed nothing and carried her back to bed. He climbed in beside her and brushed her hair away from her face. She ran her fingers over the scratchy surface of his stubble and brought his lips closer.

"I'm still a little worried Cordy will think badly of me."

"Don't worry about Cordy. She likes you. She gave us her blessing."

"Anything you don't like, tell me." He kissed her again.

She doubted there would be anything she didn't like. His kisses burned her from the inside out. Whatever his hands were capable of would turn her to ashes. She had never wanted a man so much, and it wasn't just because he was a great kisser or because he was familiar. His heart was as big as the sky. And truthfully, he wasn't the same man he was in the past. Prison had changed him, closed him off. But his kindness and integrity still shone.

She explored the muscles of his back until she had memorized each one. But his hands had remained near her face or ran up and down her arm. She eased out of the kiss and brought her lips to his neck. Her tongue left trails across his salty skin. Her lips found his collarbone while her hands continued to learn about him and what he liked. She quickly checked in for any intruding thoughts about fear or waiting. Her mind responded in silence for once. Only the desire to be with him pulsed in her brain.

"You feel good," he said.

The words gave her courage to run her fingers through his chest hair and down the front of his body. She hesitated at the top of his sweatpants but wanted to feel all of him against her and pushed on the waistband. He gripped her hand.

"Not yet." He turned so they faced each other.

"Why?" She ran her knuckles over his jaw.

"If you're not going to let me take you to a fancy hotel room or at least a cabin for just the two of us without extra ears in the house, I want to take care of you first." He ran a finger from right below her neck to her navel. Even over her shirt, her skin tingled in anticipation of more.

"You don't have to do that. I don't think I can keep my hands off you." Touching him made her heart see again.

He choked out a laugh. "I like the sound of that, but you deserve to feel special because you are."

"You think you're not good with words, but you're wrong. You always say what's on your mind." She appreciated his directness. She knew where she stood with him, eliminating any guessing. She would rather know what she was dealing with than be surprised by unspoken feelings. The unknown scared her.

"Then I'm going to say this before we go any further. How long has it been since you were with a man this way?"

She was grateful for the cover of darkness, hiding the blush on her cheeks. She hadn't had many lovers, and the sex between her and Oliver was all right, but not passionate. "Almost two years. Oliver and I had stopped having sex six months before the incident." They had been growing apart for so long, she shouldn't have been astonished when he wasn't there for her. If she had been paying attention, she would've left him sooner.

He pushed up on his elbow. "I want to make love to you the right way. Slow. Me taking care of you."

He undid the first button of her nightshirt. He pushed the fabric open and placed a kiss against her heated skin. He shifted so he was on top of her and undid the next button. His lips made circles on her skin. She needed to touch him too and tangled her fingers in his hair.

"No touching."

"Please." Her breath became short bursts of air.

"Not yet." He undid the next button. The shirt fell open, exposing her breasts. The air cooled her skin. His mouth, playful on her nipple, sent a rousing surge through her center. Every nerve was on high alert, and she arched her back for more of his taste. His other hand worked the next button until she lay there naked for him. The way she wanted to be.

His hands played her body like a good love song. The clouds that had covered her with uncertainty for so long parted and allowed in the bright promise of tomorrow. She had found her way home and had this man to thank for that. She had made so many mistakes in her life and still had managed to come full circle with him. She hadn't even known she still wanted him, but he was all she wanted.

He coaxed her to the edge with long strokes and hard kisses, but teased her back each time, not letting her fall over. Every part of body trembled and throbbed. She wouldn't last another second if he didn't give her some relief.

"Caleb?"

"Yes?" He kissed her neck while his hands tantalized her.

She took a deep breath. "I want you inside me."

He stilled and looked at her. A devilish grin crossed his face. "Whatever the lady desires."

She hadn't thought about protection but should have. She had been swept up in coming downstairs and persuading him what they were doing was okay even in Cordy's house. "Do you have a condom? Since it's been a while, I don't have any in the house."

He slid from the bed and went to the rocking chair covered with his clothes and rustled around, returning with what they needed.

He really was taking care of her in so many ways. She had come to rely on him and for a second her lungs pushed out all their air. She couldn't breathe, and her heart sputtered. What if she had relied too much? What would she do if she lost him for good? What if those men hunted him down next time? What if they came for her? *No.* Nothing bad would happen. She gathered her runaway thoughts and tied them up. She shouldn't allow her fears in bed with them. Together, she and Caleb would fix their problems.

"Hey, are you sure you're okay?" he said.

"Why wouldn't I be?"

"You went kind of stiff there for a second when I climbed back into bed."

She placed her hands on his face. Her sweet man had read

her thoughts. "I am absolutely ready for this. We belong together." She had never meant anything more.

"Then let's do this." He held her gaze; even though the room was too dark to read his expression, the connection was as strong as the oldest oak and the surest sunrise. He entered her slowly, filling her up, making everything all right, keeping her safe. The world slipped away except for the two of them and the way their bodies worked in effortlessness.

The hot desperate coil inside her rose and tightened. She willed her mind to follow it, wanting to fall off the edge into oblivion, but her mind would not obey. Her breath came in shorter bursts now. The end was close but out of reach.

He dropped his mouth to her ear. "Jump. I'll catch you."

A moan escaped her lips. He knew what she needed, which gave her the certainty to keep going. She drove her hips up to meet his and soared into the white light of her mind. She gripped his back as the waves of indulgent pleasure washed over her, drenching her in sweat and opulence. He lost control and called out her name as he joined her.

Her body was slick, but he gathered her to him, holding her close. She stayed wrapped around him until her heart returned to its normal beat.

"Do you think you can sleep now?" He ran his hand up and down her back, igniting her all over again.

She moved to see him better. "Sleep is the last thing on my mind."

His body shook with laughter.

Then he kissed her.

CHAPTER FIFTEEN

Brooklyn glided around the kitchen as if her feet were on wheels. She had been up early to take care of the alpacas, and had left Caleb's bed with some regret. He had been asleep, and she hadn't wanted to wake him. She had slid from the bed and stolen a few more glances at his well-defined body before covering him with the blankets and left. Lucy and Ethel had stayed close to her side while she filled the feeders and purred their unusual but happy sound as if they could tell she was happy too.

"You're in a chipper mood this morning." Cordy entered the kitchen in her nightgown, robe, and slippers. Her silver hair hung down her back. An impish grin pushed up her lips and she arched a questioning brow.

"Am I? I hadn't noticed." She smiled to herself. Her body still strummed from all the lovemaking last night. She couldn't wait to get him alone and do it again.

"I could hear you humming from the top of the stairs. You sounded like the alpacas. And you're swinging those hips like you're practicing for a salsa competition." Cordy grabbed a glass and filled it with water from the tap.

She shrugged and went back to scrambling eggs. She wanted to make a nice breakfast for Caleb. He must've worked up an appetite. She certainly had.

As if on cue, he hurried into the kitchen, shrugging into his jacket. He had showered, but not shaved. The two-day-old beard only added to her fantasies.

"Good morning, ladies. I'm heading out."

He hadn't mentioned anything to her about an early-morning appointment. She wanted to ask where he was going, but she wasn't his keeper. She wasn't even his girl-friend. They hadn't established a name for what they were doing. What happened last night didn't give her any right to anything. No one had spoken of a commitment other than he'd stay in town for a while.

"I made some breakfast, if you'd like to eat before you go." She reached for a plate.

"Thanks, but I don't have time. I'll be gone most of the day too." He snagged a banana off the counter. "See you later." And he pushed out the back door.

She tried to temper the disobedient emotions by pushing the eggs around the skillet. Not even a kiss goodbye. Cordy glanced at her over the rim of the water glass. Her eyebrows reached for her hairline.

"What?" She turned away in case her cheeks were flaming red.

"Well, for one, you're desecrating those eggs. And for two, I'm taking a wild guess this was not the way you saw the morning play out."

"I don't know what you're talking about." Why did that woman have to be so damn insightful?

Cordy glanced out the window. "Looks like he's walking to wherever he's going. You still have time to catch him. If you want, that is."

"He doesn't have to tell me where he's going. I'm not in

charge of him just because I gave him a place to stay until his bike is fixed."

"No, he doesn't, but a kiss goodbye would've been nice. I saw you two outside yesterday. I also heard some whispering last night. I wasn't eavesdropping." She raised both hands in the air. "I'm no Weezer River. I'll tell you that much. But I couldn't sleep and came down for a snack. I thought I heard voices. I only started down the hall when I realized it must be you two. Then I ran for the hills." She let out a laugh and held her belly until the laughter trailed off.

"I'll be right back. And not another word." She pointed at Cordy with the spatula, then hurried after Caleb.

The morning sun hadn't the chance to warm the day yet. The vibrant leaves stood out against the clear blue sky. The alpacas must've sensed her nerves and came around the barn to greet her. Lucy and Ethel shared a long piece of hay.

"Caleb, wait." She hurried down the driveway.

He stopped and turned but didn't come any closer. He was going to make her walk the whole way.

"Is everything okay?" he said when she got closer.

"That's what I wanted to ask you. You rushed out of the house. Did something happen?" She crossed her arms over her middle to ward off the chilly morning as well as the chill inside her.

He shoved his hands in his pockets. "I have some things to do in town this morning."

"You could've borrowed my car." She didn't understand this change in him. His face seemed impassive, and he clenched his jaw.

"I need to do this on my own. Plus, my bike might be ready today. If it is, I want to be able to ride it. The walk will do me some good. Clear my head."

"Clear your head from what? Last night you seemed pretty focused. Has something changed?"

"Brooklyn,…" His words died out, and his gaze drifted.

She held her breath. He was going to say he regretted what happened. He wasn't going to stay in town and try to make a go of things with her. How could she have misread him so badly? Because he had said all the right things.

"Just say it." She couldn't stand the strained silence another second.

"I'm going to look for a job. I need to be able to support myself. I have a little money, but it won't last forever. I didn't want to say anything in front of Cordy. Or to you in case my plan doesn't work out. If I can't work in town, I'm going to have to expand the search. That could take a little while to come up with something. I don't want you thinking I'm less of a man because I don't have a job."

"You were afraid to tell me you're job hunting?" She should be apologizing to him for allowing that negative voice to creep into her thoughts and make her insecure about the two of them after what they shared last night. She had come so far since last year, but still had a ways to go before she could trust her confidence again.

"It sounds kind of stupid when you say it that way. Listen, I know you could be with any man you wanted. You have it all, and I don't. I don't want anyone giving you a hard time for being with me."

She cleared the space between them, drawn by a pull she couldn't fight even if she wanted to. She slid her hands around his waist and tugged him close. "You do have the whole package, Mr. Ransom. You're kind and caring, smart, sure of yourself, and very good in bed."

He tossed his head back with a resounding laugh. "That last part might be because you don't have much to compare me to."

"He jests." She ran her fingers over his beard, enjoying his playfulness. "I don't care what anyone thinks. We aren't their

159

business. Get the job for you. I'll support whatever you do." She hoped he believed her.

He placed a kiss on her nose. "Thanks for saying that, but your father will disapprove even more if I'm a loser without a job. He's not going to like that I swept his daughter off her feet and into my bed."

The memory of him carrying her to bed last night curled her toes. She did not care that Caleb had spent the better part of a decade wandering from town to town. His world had been upended and he had been trying ever since to set it straight. He had always worked even if he did move around. He wasn't destitute, and maybe his permanent address wasn't so permanent, but having the big house with a fancy zip code, expensive cars, and the right job did not guarantee happiness or love. Money only guaranteed money problems didn't exist, and though that was a huge weight not to carry, at the end of her life, she wanted it filled with people who loved her and who she mattered to.

"Don't worry about my father. He'll come around." She planned on talking to her dad today about her and Caleb. And about the very likely possibility the men who cornered him in the parking lot were part of her uncle Huck's group.

"What are you going to do today while I'm out pounding the pavement?" He took her hand and led her down the driveway toward the street. Their slow steps echoed against the gravel. They moved as if they had nowhere to be, like they were the only two people in the world. She soaked in the trees that lined the drive and Caleb's strong profile.

"Maybe I should job hunt too, in case I can't convince Cordy to sell me the farm."

"Would you work on the orchard or go back to nursing?"

"I'm done with nursing except for the occasional stranger at the door." She winked and he laughed. "I don't know about the orchard. I never really fit in there. My cousins and my brother are more suited for the family business. I'm like the black sheep when it comes to employment at the orchard."

"Or the black alpaca."

"Funny." She had tried a few different jobs on the orchard. Her father had insisted she and Brad work there when they were teens, but no matter how hard she had attempted an orchard's job, nothing fit. "I don't know what I want to be, Caleb, if I can't have this farm."

They reached the end of the driveway. He cupped her face with his hands. "You want to be an alpaca farmer. Go back in there and convince Cordy to sell to you, even if it means taking Oliver's money. I'll try not to be too jealous."

She brought her lips to his. "You have nothing to worry about there. I'll see you tonight."

"See you." He turned onto the road. She placed her fingers against her lips, still tingling from the kiss, and watched until he turned out of sight.

Not only would she have to convince Cordy to sell her the farm, but she would have to tell her about the vandalism too. She hoped Cordy wouldn't blame Caleb for what happened. If she did, Brooklyn would tell her about what had happened to him in the parking lot of the grocery store. Whoever wanted Caleb out of town was determined, but she wouldn't allow anyone to tell her they shouldn't be together. They would stand united and fight back. Because she would not be a victim again.

She returned to the house, still vibrating from the kiss. Cordy stood in the kitchen, dressed now in her faded jeans and blue knitted cardigan with a white t-shirt underneath. The sweater was one of her creations and made from one of the lighter alpacas whose fur could be dyed.

"That's a pretty sweater." She reached past Cordy for the coffee pot.

"Thank you. I can show you how to make one if you'd like." Cordy handed her a blueberry muffin. "It's still hot."

"Was I outside that long?"

"I made the batter last night when I came downstairs." Cordy waved a hand in the air. Her bracelets jangled in response.

"I'd like to learn how to make the cardigan. Thank you for suggesting it." She split apart the hot muffin. Steam billowed right from the center. "Do you have the recipe for these? I'd like to make them too." Baking and the farm and Caleb were quickly defining home for her.

"Somewhere. I'll search for it. You know, I saw you two out there."

"Were you spying on us?" A tart blueberry exploded in her mouth.

"I wouldn't call it spying. Just observing. I know love when I see it."

"I don't know that I'd call it love just yet." She didn't want to get too far ahead of herself. He was staying in town. That was all she needed at the moment.

"That man just hightailed it out of here, but turned at the sound of your voice and hung his head until you spoke and put a smile on his face. You can deny it all you want, tell me it's too soon or whatever horseshit you want to throw, but I know what I saw. He's sticking around for you, isn't he?"

"Yes." Her heart swelled and threatened to burst like that blueberry with her declaration.

"Your father is going to have his backside in crosshairs when he finds out." Cordy poured hot water into her mug and claimed a seat at the table.

"I'll deal with him." She put the muffin down. "Listen, Cordy, about the farm—"

"Call Oliver and tell him to give you the money."

"Excuse me?"

"Watching you and Caleb reminded me of your grandfather and me when we were young. Levon would do anything to make me happy. I can see that's what Caleb wants to do for you. He knew how much this farm meant to you when I didn't. I guess I'm the fool he said I was. I'm sorry about that."

"You have nothing to be sorry for. You've helped me so much since I've been back. It was only when I thought I'd lose my home that I wanted to fight for it. You helped me speed up my decision. But are you serious? You're willing to sell the farm to me?"

"I'll call Brad and tell him to find another property. I won't deny you a chance for a lifetime of happiness. You and Caleb belong here. Love belongs here."

"You're a hopeless romantic."

"Guilty."

"I'm glad you approve of me and Caleb. That means a lot." She gripped her grandmother in a tight hug.

She did want her family's acceptance of them, but if she didn't get it, she meant what she had said. Her life was no one's business. She would not explain herself—too much.

"I've always liked him. He didn't kill SJ. The naysayers of this town wanted someone to blame for the death of one of their celebrities because no one wanted to admit a Wilde was less than perfect. Those same people turn a blind eye to Huck's narrow-minded group."

"It's not always easy being a part of my family. We have our skeletons just like everyone except some of us don't have to own up to them—like Huck. While some of us are still judged. All the whispers I got when I returned to town..." The memories of people gossiping behind their hands with wide stares in her direction as she entered a store or walked the orchard still hurt. "The rumor mill couldn't churn fast enough with news that a Wilde had been assaulted, ended up divorced, and had returned home to lick her wounds. I didn't want to go out for fear of seeing someone who would point and laugh."

"But you did, with your head held high. The way I knew you would. I'm proud of you, and I'm glad you want my farm. I'd rather it stays as a place to welcome families and offer love to the alpacas."

"Thank you. I won't let you down." Now was the time to tell her about the vandalism. "Cordy, there's something I need to tell you."

Cordy moved the muffins from the cooling rack to a ceramic plate painted with blue and yellow flowers. "Really? What's that?"

"Two days ago, someone vandalized the barn. The alpacas weren't hurt."

Cordy's hand stopped midair. The color drained from her face. "Thank goodness no one hurt those babies. What happened? Why didn't you say something sooner?"

"I should have. Time got away from me with all that's been happening. Anyway, I'm telling you now. The worst part was the tools were broken. I think whoever did it wanted to scare me. They weren't trying to do real damage." At least that's what she hoped, because they could've done so much worse, but what would this person do now when word traveled about her and Caleb?

Cordy dropped back in the chair with a thud. "Well, my word. Who in Pete's name would do something like that? Did you report it?"

"I didn't see the point. Caleb had it cleaned up in record time and nothing was stolen. I think Officer Vetter could be involved. He's after Caleb. He wants to pin the Holloway robbery on him."

"Of course, he does, that intolerant weasel of a man. We

can't allow that to happen." Cordy went back to arranging her muffins on the plate with a firm nod of her chin.

"You're still okay with Caleb staying here?"

"Do I resemble a woman who throws out a man because of the opinion of another?"

She bit her lip not to laugh. Her grandmother had a way with words. "Absolutely not. I'm sorry I suggested it. But seriously, Cordy, I don't want anything bad to happen to you or the alpacas. In fact, I hate to say this, but me being with Caleb is actually a reason to sell to Brad after all." She may have just shot herself in the foot with that revelation, but the truth was the truth no matter how awkward.

"We don't back down from bullies. And I meant every word I said. This place is about love, and that's you and Caleb. You'll build a good life here, and live for years surrounded by this pasture and these trees and hills. When you're my age, you'll pass this farm to your own children."

"I wish you weren't going to move so far. I want you around. I need you around to remind me I'm good enough as I am."

"You never forget you're good enough. You're my grand-daughter." Cordy waved an arm in the air. "Besides, you can come and visit. Come for Christmas. I plan on being out there by then."

"So soon?" That was only a couple of months away.

"This is the next stage of my life. I've always trusted that voice in my heart. It's never steered me wrong. I think you're beginning to trust yours too."

"I think you're right." When she thought about the farm, the alpacas, and now Caleb, her insides opened and set her free.

She was finally on the right path. Nothing could stop her.

~

Caleb opened the door to the service station of Hafrey's Garage. The bell above the door jangled the announcement of his arrival. The inside didn't include much more than a glass case that held some items for car cleaning that Jameson sold, and the cash register on top. Jameson also made available a couple of dirty plastic chairs for patrons to wait for their cars.

A calendar hung on the paneled wall behind the case along with a few local awards for being the best garage in Hunterdon County and pictures of local sports teams that Jameson had sponsored. The place smelled of grease and dirt and sweat. He rang the bell on the counter, unsure if anyone would hear him in the garage because of the noisy power tools and the yelling above the radio turned to a club station.

"Coming," Jameson shouted from the back. He came through the doorway wiping his greasy hands on an even greasier towel. "Hey, Caleb. I was just about to call you. Your bike is ready."

"That's great. Thanks. I'll settle up with you." He dug his wallet out of his jacket pocket. At least he wouldn't have to walk back to the farm. The temperature had dropped since he left Brooklyn earlier. Fall was sticking around. The days grew shorter, giving dark nights the upper hand. He would have to tell Brooklyn to be more careful if she went out alone at night. And he would too. He couldn't afford another motorcycle accident.

"What happened to your face?"

"Oh, that. I got mugged in the parking lot of the supermarket a few nights ago." The pain was all but gone, and after last night with Brooklyn, his mind was on other things besides his injuries.

"It was those bastards, wasn't it? Huck Wilde's men?" Jameson slammed the towel down.

"I don't know, but I think so. What made you guess that?"

"Everyone in town comes through here for one reason or another. There's been talk about what happened to you, your wipeout that is. They never said who it was, but a few of the guys had themselves a good laugh about it in my earshot." Jameson tapped the cash register with his finger. The drawer popped open with a ding.

"Glad I could be the brunt of their joke." He handed over his credit card. Fixing the bike would max it out. He would try not to worry about money; once he started working, he'd be on his feet again. Brooklyn deserved a man who could at least support himself. After seeing her ex and his expensive car, she would be downgrading to him, and he didn't want her ever regretting her choice.

"Sorry. I shouldn't have said anything."

"Forget it." Those bastards could laugh all they wanted. But he never wanted Brooklyn to be embarrassed by him. She deserved the best. He would prove himself worthy, somehow.

"Hey, um…I was wondering if I could ask you something?" He cleared his throat. Asking for work never got any easier even after the ten years he'd been doing it. Most bosses wanted to know his experience and check references. He had moved around so much. He often didn't have a lot to tell the next boss which could sometimes result in working places he would rather not. All that had to change. He would need a good job now, something with stability.

"Sure." Jameson's smile split open his face.

"Any chance you need help around here?"

"Are you looking or looking for someone else?" The smile faltered.

He wanted to turn and go, but plunged on. "Me. I'm planning to stay in town for a while. I need some work. I'm good with my hands. I've worked garages before." He'd worked garages, kitchens, and landscaping. He went where the money was and learned quickly.

"Then just temporary work until you're ready to move on?"

"I have no plans to move on anytime soon." He only hoped the men who had started coming for him would back off. He might not be so lucky. More likely, he'd have to fight them, and he didn't want to do that. Brooklyn shouldn't be with a man who used his fists.

"Look, man, I'd love to help you out, but I can't take a chance right now. If you started working here, I could lose business or worse."

"I didn't take you for someone who backed down easily."

"I'm not up for fighting the Brotherhood of Watchmen. It's a no-win situation. I've got a business to think about and my dad who needs his full-time home aid. If I can't afford to pay for that, then my dad will end up in a state funded facility. I'm sorry, but I can't risk it."

"I understand." Which he did...but didn't. "I'll keep looking."

"I'm sorry, Caleb. I really like you, but Vetter has it in for you. He's got too much influence in this town. He's going to come down on anyone who helps you. That includes Brooklyn and Cordy. I'm not sure the Wildes' reach could stop him, if you know what I mean."

A phone started ringing. Jameson pulled it out of the pocket of his uniform shirt. "I have to get this. I really am sorry. Your bike is on the side of the garage."

He went in search of his motorcycle and found her parked at the edge of the lot. When he had been in the county jail before they took him to the state prison, Huck Wilde had come to see him. Huck had stared at him through the bars with hate in his beady eyes and told him he finally had what was coming to him. That people like him didn't deserve to walk the streets with the likes of the Huck Wildes of the world. He had never forgotten that voice. The man that had spoken while the others kicked and beat him had the same voice. Huck had been the leader that night. That was why he believed Brad knew something about the accident. Huck liked to brag. He must have bragged to Brad, and he would find out.

A cloud passed over the sun, turning the color off on the day. A wind swirled and brought a chill with it. The hairs on the back of his neck stood up. He turned. His gaze searched the area. Someone was watching him. He had learned to trust that intuition in prison. Eyes in the back of his head and all that.

Officer Vetter stood across the street about a block down. There was no missing the uniform and the black shiny hair. He kept his gaze on the man to make sure he knew he had been spotted. Had Vetter been one of the men in the grocery store parking lot who beat him up? Why was he even guessing? Of course, he was.

"Caleb." Someone shouted his name. He took his gaze away from Vetter, and his heart sunk.

Brooklyn waved to him from across the street. Her smile was wide enough to power Main Street. She stood closer to Vetter than he did and gave herself away. His sweet innocent Brooklyn who wouldn't notice Officer Vetter watching her and calculating what that wave meant. His beautiful lady, who had been through something traumatic, still didn't realize that evil lurked everywhere. Even in Candlewood Falls. Maybe he was being paranoid, but prison had a way of doing that to a man. There was paranoia and his attack in the parking lot, the vandalism to the barn, as well as his accident. Now he had been told a job in Candlewood Falls would be impossible to obtain.

He hurried across the street to stop her from anymore displays. She leaned up to kiss him, but he put his hands up and stepped back. A dark confusion passed over her face.

"Not here," he said through gritted teeth. "You're making a scene." He stole a glance down the street. Vetter still stared in their direction.

"You don't want—"

"I said not here, Brooklyn. For once, just listen to me." He turned before she could say anything else and he could witness the hurt in her eyes. His abruptness was for her own safety.

He retrieved his motorcycle, kicked her over, and soaked in the roar of her engine. He didn't dare risk a glance in Brooklyn's direction. Hopefully, she stormed off and that would give Vetter enough to believe that whatever was going on between him and Brooklyn wasn't good. He couldn't allow Vetter to hurt her because of him.

A fire burned in his belly as he navigated the streets. He didn't want to fight anymore. In fact, he would prefer to be left alone, but men like Vetter and Huck Wilde didn't care about that. They saw him as a threat for all the wrong reasons, and they wanted that threat removed. He saw no other option but to make his position known. He would not back down. Not to them. Not to anyone.

He pulled in at Wilde Orchards. Even the shift in the weather hadn't deterred customers from coming out. The place was full of visitors who wanted pumpkins, apples, and donuts. A sign boasted the weekly haunted orchard for the month of October. That event had been going on for years and brought people for miles. This place was a gold mine. No wonder Brad had plans to expand.

He parked his bike and stalked out to the fields where he would most likely find men working. He hoped to find Huck, but he would settle for Brad. They hadn't spoken since the last time he had asked Brad to keep an eye on Brooklyn. He wasn't even sure if Brad had checked on her. Not that he should be surprised. Brad didn't want to listen to him, but he had better today.

He found Brad messing around with trees that didn't look open to the public. The guy from the forklift the other day squatted near him, checking the soil.

"Hey, Brad." He kept a good distance and waited for him to look up.

Brad's head snapped up at the sound of his name, but the smile fell off his face when he realized where the call came from.

"Are you still in town? I thought you would've left by now." He swaggered over, so used to being on top of the world. Men like Brad Wilde got their way with little effort. He had been born into a prestigious family that oozed respect and money. He hadn't had to fight for anything and believed he never would. Caleb hoped for his sake he never did.

"I need to speak to your uncle Huck. Is he here?"

"Someplace. Why do you want to speak to him?" Brad shook his hair out of his face.

"Just tell me where he is."

"He's someplace on the hundred acres. Good luck finding him." Brad turned to walk away.

"He wants to hurt Brooklyn." He had no other choice but to use that piece of information even if he wasn't entirely sure it was true. Vetter would definitely hurt Brooklyn, but he still wanted to believe Huck would have more sense than to do something to his own niece.

Brad stopped. He turned with deliberation. His lip curled in a snarl. His blue eyes had turned the color of an angry ocean. "You shouldn't go around accusing men of things they wouldn't do. The only person my sister could get hurt from is you."

He started to think that might be true. "The other night I got jumped in the supermarket parking lot. One voice stood out to me. Huck's. I would know that voice anywhere because he had come to jail to threaten me. His voice was the one who had told me to stay away from Brooklyn the other night. What more do you need me to tell you? You can't be so stupid you don't know what Huck is a part of around here."

Brad glared at him with a clenched jaw. Caleb waited. If he said a word, Brad might turn around and go back to his trees, but if he held Brad's angry gaze and stayed silent, Brad might give in and take him to Huck.

"Hey, Brad, what gives?" the guy from the forklift said, breaking the tension.

"I need about ten minutes, Raf. I'll be back." Brad stomped past him, yanking a walkie-talkie off the side of his belt. He followed on Brad's heels.

"Huck, meet me at the store. Someone is here who wants to speak with you."

A crackling came through. "Who is it?" Huck's recognizable gravelly voice made the bile in his stomach rise.

"Just meet me there." Brad switched off the device.

They rounded the corner of the store, bringing them to the front. A few customers lingered in the flower garden, taking pictures and drinking cider. Benches, flanked by pots of purple flowers, waited for someone to sit and enjoy the view. No one paid any attention to them, so caught up in their own lives. He preferred it that way—anonymous, unseen.

Huck came from the other side of the store. He was tall like all the Wilde guys seemed to be. But he was older with hunched shoulders and wiry arms. His skin sagged around his chin and his hair had turned white and thinned out. His gait was slow with a hitch every time he led with his left leg. Maybe at one time, Huck Wilde was a scary man, but not today. Not for him.

"What the hell does he want?" Huck stopped in his tracks.

Brad found a spot off to the side of the store, where some bushes grew tall, where customers couldn't hear them and positioned himself between, Huck and him. "He has something he wants to say to you."

"And you bothered me about it?" Huck's eyebrows shot up.

"It concerns Brooklyn," Brad said.

Huck crossed his arms over his chest and nodded his head. He wasn't sure if that was an indicator to begin, but he sure as hell was going to take it as if it were.

"I'm not leaving town. And I want you to stay away from Brooklyn. If you even try to hurt her, I will come for you in the middle of the night when you're all alone."

"Are you threatening me?" Huck lunged forward. Brad put a hand on Huck's shoulder to stop him.

"I'm promising you that I won't let you hurt her anymore. Tell your men to back off. That stunt you pulled at the barn was too far. Your problem is with me, not her. And I'm here to tell you your problem isn't going away." He willed his heart to slow, but it beat like a racehorse's, threatening to come clean through his chest.

"I don't know what in Sam's hell you're talking about. I wouldn't send anyone after my niece."

"I heard you the night I got jumped."

"I wish I was there, boy, to see you get your ass whooped, but I wasn't." Huck smirked.

"Ransom, what do you mean by stunt at the *barn*?" Brad said.

"Someone vandalized the barn the other night, breaking stuff and disrupting the alpacas. It was a threat to get rid of me."

"You sent someone to destroy Cordy's barn, Uncle

Huck?" Disbelief rang through Brad's words like a siren.

"Hell no. I wouldn't hurt my family. Now, him, yes." Huck turned to him. "If you left town, there'd be no reason for Brooklyn to be involved in your mess. No one wants you here. You stink up the place. You shouldn't have stopped at the bar the other night. You'd be long gone by now, and we could go back to forgetting you ever existed. And if you ever threaten me again, I'll take your damn head off with one hand." Huck stormed off as best he could with that leg, not waiting for a reply.

Acid burned in his stomach. He wasn't in prison anymore, but it sure felt like it. He wanted to punch someone or something, but fought the urge with everything he had. He needed to be a better man.

"I don't think he's lying," Brad said. "My uncle is a lot of things, but he's not a liar. Are you sure it was him you heard?"

"Yeah." Maybe he had heard wrong. He was getting the crap beat out of him at the time. He had been focused on not dying.

"Did you see anyone the other night at the barn?" Brad said.

"Brooklyn found the mess in the morning. Whoever had done it was long gone." Whoever had vandalized the barn must have been in and out quickly. The alpacas would have given them away with all the screeching. Or this person knew how to make the alpacas feel comfortable, had been around the animals before.

"Could've been the same people who robbed Mrs. Holloway," Brad said.

They had no proof as to who went through there, and he wished they did. He couldn't believe he might actually be agreeing with Brad. "I suppose. But why not take anything that was valuable instead of breaking it?"

"I don't know. Maybe whoever came to the barn was leaving you a message. Take Huck's advice. Get out of town, Caleb. Brooklyn deserves better than you." Brad took off in the direction his uncle had gone.

He headed for the parking lot and almost bumped into a family standing together. A man, woman, and two kids. The woman, probably the mother, broke a donut in half, squatted down, and handed each child one. The children laughed as they bit into the donuts and powdered sugar burst into the air. The dad snapped photos with his phone. Caleb sucked in a breath.

He wanted that, a family and a place to call home. For a brief second, he thought he may have found it with Brooklyn. She made him feel alive instead of a man just marking time, waiting for the end to come, which he thought had when he fell off his bike. In a crazy way she made him feel safe, complete even. She thought she needed security, but she was wrong. He needed it, but he couldn't have it here. Huck would never leave him alone. Vetter would never stop either.

Brad was right. Brooklyn deserved better than a man who would spend his life looking over his shoulder, wondering who was sizing him up, who was thinking he was no good, who was out to get him. A man who couldn't even get hired for a job—not even from his friend Malbec River.

Caleb jumped on his bike, revved the engine just because he could, and left the orchard in the dust. The time had come to move on.

CHAPTER SIXTEEN

Brooklyn seethed all morning while she ran some errands. She didn't understand what was wrong with Caleb. He had seemed so angry with her with his cold eyes and clenched jaw. It was as if she didn't recognize him at all in that moment. He was a completely different man from the one who left her just this morning. Something must have happened. Had someone else threatened him? She hoped not. Was he prone to mood swings? She didn't think so, but how well did she really know him? They hadn't spoken at all about his life. He never wanted to. What had prison done to him? And did she really want to know?

She would worry about Caleb later. She needed to find her father now and discuss who might have attacked Caleb in the parking lot. Every place she had stopped this morning, she had sought out her dad because when she had tried his cell phone, it was turned off. Like usual. She had even started at his cabin, but he wasn't home. She went to the orchard, but no one had seen him. She stopped in at the library where he sometimes went to read or use a computer if he wanted to do research. She peeked in all the stores on Main Street even though she didn't expect to see him at Witchy Woman where customers received palm readings. She had highly doubted that he would be at Vivian's Hair Salon because he cut his own hair, and sure enough he wasn't.

The only possible place left was the Green Bean. Even this would be a waste of time, but she was here and could use a strong coffee anyway.

Dad sat in the corner all alone with a newspaper in his hand and a white mug on the table. Most likely plain black coffee. She tempered the anger for having to look everywhere for him and zagged around the tables to accomplish her mission.

"I never expected to see you here." She moved the paper, forcing him to look at her.

His laid-back smile spread across his face and brightened his blue eyes. The same eyes she and Brad had. Dad folded the paper and pointed to the other chair, oblivious to any emotion on her face. And she was pretty sure there had to be one or two because poker wasn't her game. "This is a nice surprise. Sit with me a while," he said.

She pulled out the chair and dropped down. "What are you doing here?" She kept her voice low so none of the employees or customers would hear her. She didn't need to give anyone more reason to gossip about her.

"Every once in a while, I like to visit the world I used to live in so I can remember why I love my quiet life so much." He folded his hands on the table. His smile ignited a small dimple in his cheek.

"Funny, Dad. You go to the orchard almost every day to work. Isn't that a part of the world you used to live in?"

"Not the same. I stay out in the fields with the men and women. I like dirt between my fingers. I couldn't work those fancy registers or create publicity packages, if my life depended on it."

"Dad, I've seen you do both." Her father pretended he didn't understand modern technology or society's advancement, but he did. He watched everyone and everything, absorbing knowledge the way cotton absorbed moisture.

He put a finger to his lips and winked. "Don't tell anyone. So, what brings you here?"

"You." She had been so determined to find him and tell him about her new relationship with Caleb. She wanted her father's blessing, but after what had happened on the sidewalk this morning, she wasn't sure if she should say anything yet. She would have to stick to the other matter for now and wait to see what Caleb had to say for his reaction.

"Me?"

"I was looking all over town for you. You don't have your cell phone on you, do you?" The conversation would have been easier over the phone, but she really had wanted a reason to see her dad. She also wanted to see his face when she told him she was happy with Caleb. But Caleb went and threw a wrench into those plans.

He patted his pockets. "Nope. Forgot it."

"Dad, it doesn't do you any good at your cabin and probably not charged. Brad and I got that for you so we could reach you if we needed you or you could reach us."

"Do you need something, Cheeks?"

She sighed at the use of the nickname. She was a grown woman with an actual name, but she understood that she was his child and let it go. "I need some advice."

"I'll do my best to help."

Of course, he would. She was rattled not because he called her Cheeks, but because of Caleb and her strong feelings for him. "How do you know when you've found the right person to be with?"

He sat back and scratched at his beard. She could almost see the wheels turning in his mind. He and her mother hadn't had a whirlwind love affair. They didn't have a romantic story that made a heart swoon. They had dated, had sex; she ended up pregnant with twins, and he did the right thing by offering to marry her. Her mother had only said yes because Dad was a Wilde.

"Are you thinking of reconciling with Oliver?" His eyes grew wide.

"Absolutely not. Who told you he was in town? It's barely been twenty-four hours." She had called Oliver this morning and told him to draw up papers or whatever he wanted to make the deal legit. That was the very thing she was going to share with Caleb when she saw him come out of Jameson's place. But when he had marched across the street with fury defining his face, the words had dried up.

Dad choked out a laugh. "You should know by now there are very few secrets in Candlewood Falls. All the real ones are buried deep. So, it's not Oliver. Then why is he here?"

"He's going to lend me money. It looks like I'm buying the farm from Cordy." She had hoped Cordy had spoken to Brad. She had said she would make it her first priority today.

"What did Brad say?"

"I'll tell you what I said." Her brother appeared like a demon in a devil possession movie. Indignation creased his brows. He blocked the light from the large glass window with his broad shoulders and big head. She craned her neck to see him, but then dropped her gaze. Whatever he was pissed about, she wasn't sure she wanted to hear. She had had enough of annoyed men for one day. Brad grabbed a chair with force from a nearby table, startling the woman at the table, then spun it around and straddled it.

"Hey, son."

"Hi, Dad. I came looking for you, Brooklyn, because your boyfriend has his head up his ass, but before I could find you, Cordy called. Why do you want the farm?"

Some customers at neighboring tables had turned to watch the show that was about to unfold. Being on display made her heart race and her thighs sweat. She wanted to pull her sweater up over her head.

"Keep your voice down," she said.

"Ask me if I care right now." His eyebrows climbed into his hairline.

"Now, what's this about her boyfriend?" Her father smirked.

"I'll get to that in a second, Dad." Brad turned to her. "Why didn't you come to me yourself if it's so important to you to own the farm? You don't think I would've understood that?"

"No, actually, I don't. I'm not trying to compete with you. I just want to keep my home and those animals." She should have called him herself if only for the reason to avoid a scene.

"You never stick with anything. What makes you think you'll stick with the farm?"

"Because I love it there. Why does it matter? You could plant trees anywhere." Her head hurt from all the arguing and worrying. If she failed at the farm, she would only have herself to blame, then everyone could tell her they told her so.

"I could probably find land somewhere else to plant more trees. I wish you had come to me right away instead of going to Cordy first. I would've backed off for you. You're my twin. I'd do anything for you."

His sudden change of demeanor took all the anger out of her sails. Guilt played her like a fiddle. She had been afraid to ask for help from her brother because she thought she was alone in all of this, but that wasn't the case. She had pulled herself away from her family this past year to protect herself and to protect them.

"I'm sorry. I should have spoken to you. I didn't want to

say anything, even to Cordy, until I knew I had the money. And she told me no at first. Buying the farm didn't seem possible until this morning." She had hoped to work the farm with Caleb. That seemed like part of the dream to her, the two of them side by side, caring for the animals, expanding the business. The look on his face earlier, as if he were disgusted by her waving to him, turned her stomach. Probably a good thing she had forgotten to get that coffee she thought she wanted.

"What changed her mind?" Dad said.

"I think she realized how important staying there was to me." She left out the part about her and Caleb and how Cordy saw herself and Levon in the young love.

Her fingers itched to text him and make him tell her what that scene on the sidewalk was all about, but the conversation would be better had in person. That would have to wait until later whether she liked it or not.

"Why are you dating Caleb Ransom?" Brad said.

"This I want to hear," Dad said.

"We're not dating." They hadn't defined anything officially. Now she wasn't sure she wanted to or he still wanted to. "And even if we were, it's none of your damn business, Bradford. I don't answer to you." She loved her brother, but he always needed to be in charge, and he was good at it. If she were being honest, she was jealous. Brad had always known he wanted to run the orchard from the time they were in middle school. He had drive and determination. She had floundered, trying to find her way. Until now.

"Will you answer your father then? Are you and Caleb dating?" A hurt crossed Dad's face.

"I don't know what's happening yet. I like him. He likes me. And before you say it, I don't care about his past. The only thing that matters is the here and now. I need coffee." She got up, not waiting for a response and stood in line. She needed a minute to catch her breath. Telling her family about her love life shouldn't seem so hard, but it was. She wanted their approval as much as she wanted them to leave her choices alone.

She returned with a coffee for her and Brad as a peace offering.

"Thanks. Whatever Caleb is to you, he stormed onto the orchard demanding to talk to Huck."

"About what?" Dad leaned back in his chair and crossed his arms over his broad chest. He narrowed his eyes and creased his brow. He and Brad looked so much alike sometimes she had to blink to figure out who was standing there.

"When did he do that?" she said.

"I don't remember. Sometime before lunch. I finished up the grafting with Raf on some trees, had a few fires to put out, then Cordy called me. You didn't answer your cell, so I had someone over at the police station ping your phone. Then I came here."

"You had no right to do that." Again, he had a constant need to control everything. It was no wonder he couldn't keep a relationship for any length of time.

"It's no different than those apps that track your phone," Brad said, as if that explained everything.

"Is nothing sacred here?" Her hands flew up in frustration.

"It's Candlewood Falls, sis. Where everybody knows your business." Brad smirked.

"Will you two stop your bickering? What did Caleb say to Huck?" Concern laced her father's voice like a sticky spiderweb. She wasn't sure who he worried about, Caleb or Huck.

"Caleb told Huck to keep his merry men away from you or Caleb was coming for them. Brooks, Ransom's not the kind of man you should be involved with."

"I don't need you to tell me who I can or can't get

involved with. Did it occur to you that maybe Huck is involved? He hates Caleb because of who he is, and that's wrong. Caleb is a good man who's had a hard life. Maybe you could extend some kindness and compassion toward him instead of sitting there judging him."

She didn't really know what Caleb was up to. But almost in an instant, his behavior earlier made some sense. He thought she was in danger by being seen with him. Someone had to be watching, only she hadn't seen who. Possibly the same person who vandalized the barn, and for some reason Caleb had connected it to Huck.

Brad pushed off the chair and returned it to the table with an apology to the woman still sitting there. "Brooks, I don't know what this guy is involved with, but you should stay away from him. I don't want you getting hurt again." He fist-bumped Dad and walked out.

"I never thought he'd give me the farm. He wants to expand the orchard more than anything."

"Maybe not anything." Her dad arched a brow. "He's too much like me and doesn't say how he feels."

"I'll talk to him later and apologize again. Maybe he can have a few acres for trees. I don't need all fifteen. The alpacas would be happy with just two." She wanted more than two in case she added alpacas to the family. And she wanted space for couples to host their weddings, but shaving off a few acres for Brad wouldn't hurt anything.

"That sounds like a nice compromise. Do you want to get out of here? I'm ready for some fresh air." Dad gathered up his paper and his garbage and indicated she should follow him.

"Dad, can you talk to Huck about Caleb?" They walked to the public parking lot. The day remained cloudy and cold. The damp air seeped through her coat and into her bones. She wrapped her arms around her middle to keep in the heat.

"And say what?"

"Tell Huck to stay away from him. Why does he hate him so much?" She knew deep down exactly why Huck hated Caleb. It was stupid and petty. Huck thought he was better than Caleb because Caleb came from nothing, had to fight and scrape his way through the world, and Caleb wasn't a Wilde.

"Are you going to be with him now? Is he the person you wanted advice about?" Dad pulled out the keys to his truck and palmed them in his fist.

"What if Caleb and I are together? Can you accept him?" And if she wasn't with him, then there would be nothing to worry about.

"What if I can't?"

"I don't want it to come to that. Especially now that I'm going to stay in town for good. I would like to have your blessing, but I'll still be with him even if you disapprove." Those words hurt her to say. She wanted her father involved in every part of her life.

"You believe he really didn't kill SJ."

"He was exonerated."

"On a technicality. That doesn't mean he didn't throw the punch that sent SJ to an early grave."

"He says that's not what happened, and I believe him. SJ had plenty of other people who wanted to fight him. Huck hates Caleb because he needs someone to blame. He doesn't want SJ's reputation of being a drunk to be attached to the family. It goes against the viewpoint of that stupid group this town lets him have. They are hateful."

"That they are. I don't know when my brother decided he was better than another man. We weren't raised that way. What makes you and Caleb think it's Huck who's after him?"

"I can't think of another person in town who would go out of his way to get Caleb run out. He blames Caleb for SJ's death. Since Caleb's been back, he's been in a motorcycle accident, beaten in the parking lot of the supermarket, and the barn was vandalized. Doesn't that seem strange to you? SJ died twelve years ago. Who else would still harbor that much hate?"

"You didn't tell me about the barn. Were you hurt?"

"No, just some things were broken. Mostly, the alpacas were upset."

"I'll poke around and see if I can find anything out. I want you to watch your back. Whoever is after him, might come looking for you."

"Don't worry, Daddy. I know better now. No one is going to surprise me in a dark alley again."

Brooklyn shoved the knitting needles and the yarn back into the gray and white bag. A needle slipped and stabbed her. She stuck her finger in her mouth to stop the throb and the pin drop of blood. She would never get the hang of this knitting nonsense. It wasn't nonsense. Her hands didn't seem to know how to make anything. She had studied the directions. Yet, knitting was harder than she had imagined and required a patience she didn't have at the moment. Her mind wandered all night back to Caleb and because of that she had dropped several stitches and had to start over. Making a simple headband out of alpaca fleece might as well be as hard as open-heart surgery.

The other women in Cordy's knitting circle stood over by the refreshment table. They met twice a month upstairs above the yarn store Knit For Your Life. These women of varying ages and backgrounds had been meeting here for what seemed like decades. Members had come and gone over the years, but the tradition remained. Over skeins of yarn, they toasted happy moments and offered shoulders in time of need. This group was more than just a craft club. They had become friends. Something she didn't have any of these days besides her grandmother. She would need to change that now that she was staying in Candlewood Falls permanently.

The lady crafters had all cried when Cordy announced her decision to move to Arizona, but they had also cheered when she told them Brooklyn would be taking her place.

They stood with paper cups in their hands and pieces of chocolate cake on plates and squealed like alpacas about the projects they worked on tonight. They were all smiles and accomplishments with their scarves, blankets, and hats completed as if they had earned their medical degree. At this point, obtaining a medical degree would be easier than trying to make a blanket. But the alpaca fleece was soft and delicious against her hands. That was the only consolation.

She grabbed her tote and purse and tapped Cordy on the shoulder. "I'm going to head home." Her hands and arms ached from holding the knitting needles. Every muscle in her neck clenched from the stressful work. Knitting was supposed to be relaxing, but not for her. She wanted to be cocooned in the comfort of her home and Caleb's arms, but she wasn't so sure about him. He hadn't responded to any of her texts. Whatever had had him so upset this morning, she hoped had passed, and he would be willing to talk about it.

"Oh, are you sure you don't want to stay and have some cake? Flo made it herself." Cordy waved a cake-filled fork at her.

"No, thank you. I'm tired."

"And frustrated." Cordy brushed her hair behind her shoulder. "You'll get the hang of it."

"But not in time for you to leave. How will I make the stuff we sell in the store the way you do?"

"You'll send it out. It will cost you, but you might be able to make it up in volume. Have extra pieces made and sell them at the orchard. They have all that foot traffic. And start offering scarves as an idea for wedding favors. Brides will pay top dollar for that kind of thing."

"Why didn't you do any of this before?"

"Didn't need to."

That didn't make her feel any better. She might actually fail before she even got started. When she got home, she would pour a glass of wine and run a bath. With a little self-indulgence under her belt, she'd be ready to have that conversation with Caleb and maybe actually believe she could make the farm more successful than Cordy. She didn't have the benefit of a second income the way Cordy and Grampy had. For a brief second, she had thought she and Caleb could end up like her grandparents, but she wasn't so sure now.

"I'll see you at home." She pulled Cordy into a quick hug. "Don't eat too much cake."

"I'm going to eat the whole damn thing." Cordy threw her head back and laughed.

Her grandmother was a piece of work and she loved that about her. Cordy had a way of living life, and she needed to remember how to do the same. Well, maybe she was trying. The farm would be hers, and that had been an unsuspecting surprise. This thing with Caleb had her head turned around. Last night had been special. She didn't want that to be over before it even started.

Brooklyn took the steps down to the door, leading to the parking lot, the women's laughter fading as she moved farther away. The other side of the window was dark. The sun set earlier and earlier this time of year. That was the only thing she didn't like about fall. In a few weeks, the sun would set at five o'clock. She preferred to be home by dark, if she was alone. She wasn't sure if she'd ever get over that feeling. Last winter she had barely left the house.

She dug out her phone and video-called Caleb. She didn't want to text. She needed to see his face. He didn't answer. She tried to call him this time, hoping to at least leave a voicemail.

"This is Caleb. Leave a message or don't. Up to you." The beep went off.

"Hey, it's me. I'm leaving the knitting group and coming home." She pushed out into the night air, her keys in her free hand. If an attacker was watching for a vulnerable target, someone on the phone would be a less likely candidate. "I haven't had any dinner if you'd like to grab a bite." She wanted to sound as if she was having a conversation and not just leaving a message.

The tote and purse slid off her shoulder to her elbow as she tried to talk into the phone without dropping it. "I really need to talk to you when I get there. In about ten minutes." She stated the time because that indicated someone would be waiting for her and worried if she didn't show. All things she had learned since last year.

She hit the button to pop the trunk. The phone fell out of her hand. The bags slid off her wrist and tumbled into the parking lot, spilling the colorful yarn and the metal needles like a child's overturned toy box.

Someone grabbed her from behind. One arm clamped her around the waist and tossed her to the ground. She landed on her back with a bounce, the air leaving her lungs. Her keys went flying. A scream paralyzed in her throat.

Not again.

CHAPTER SEVENTEEN

Caleb parked his bike and stepped onto the boardwalk. The temperature at the shore had to be twenty degrees colder than back in Candlewood Falls. He shivered inside his jacket. He had driven for over two hours and wound up at the last stop on the Garden State Parkway. Now his back ached and his soul hurt.

With every mile he had hoped to figure out what to do. Did he stay with Brooklyn and build a life with her, or did he leave town and let her build a life worth living?

He leaned against the metal railing. The waves crashed and retreated only to come back and crash again. He wished he had that kind of persistence.

The farther away from Brooklyn he drove, the more he wanted to be with her. She had soothed the raw nerves that always tortured him. She didn't judge him. She had so much love to give, and she had wanted to give it to him.

And he had wanted her to love him. Because when she looked up at him with those big eyes and smiled, the world righted itself. He was whole when he was with her. How was he going to be able to walk away from that after finally finding what he needed and more importantly what he wanted?

He checked his phone. She had called and texted several times during the day, but nothing in the last few hours. She was probably pissed at him, and with every right. He had acted like an ass this afternoon, afraid that something would happen to her. He should have just explained what he thought he saw. And then he had gotten spooked and took off on his long ride.

He had allowed the negative voices in his head to win. He wasn't good enough or worthy enough. No one would love him.

But that might not be completely true. She hadn't said the words, *I love you*, but she had trusted him to make love to her. That meant something. A big something for her and him too. He wasn't in the habit of sleeping around, and he would never take for granted the gift she had given him. He should trust her and not the voices. Too bad he had to drive to the end of the state to figure it out. He should have been able to see it and be brave enough to say it. Brave like she was. Brooklyn was the bravest person he knew.

He had walked to the end of the boardwalk. He had a decision to make. Be brave and go back or keep running? He would never outrun his past. He hadn't been able to yet. Brooklyn was offering him a chance to face the future.

He hit the button to call Brooklyn. The call went to voicemail. "Hey. I'm sorry I was a jerk today. I'll be home in a couple of hours. I'll explain everything." And hopefully she'd still want him.

~

Brooklyn wasted no time. She wasn't going to be a victim again. She scrambled onto her feet, ready to run. The man grabbed her ankle and yanked her to the ground. The wind went out of her with a whoosh, and her chin hit the pavement, rattling her teeth. The man flipped her onto her back. She stared up at a black mask with the eyes cut out. The person stared back at her with a vacantness in his gaze.

"You were warned to stay away from Ransom." His raspy voice turned the water in her belly to ice.

He punched her in the gut. She turned on her side, coughing and gagging. Her fingers grasped something cold and thin. *The knitting needles.* She gripped them and swung with all her might. The needles pierced through the man's shirt and stuck deep in his shoulder.

He reared back and hollered, trying to pull the needles out. Blood ran over his shirt and down his arm.

She struggled to her feet.

"Oh my God. Someone help. Joan, call the police." Cordy's voice echoed in the distance as if she were coming toward Brooklyn through a tunnel.

The man took off into the dark. His footsteps faded away. Cordy gathered her in her arms and held her close.

"You're safe now," Cordy said.

She wanted to believe that was true. But she wasn't. Not even in Candlewood Falls. Because someone wanted her and Caleb apart and would stop at nothing until they had their way.

CHAPTER EIGHTEEN

Brooklyn curled up on the sofa in her living room and pulled the blanket over her. The soft alpaca fleece made a cocoon of protection. She wanted to forget about the whole night. She had also wanted Caleb's arms around her, but he wasn't here. His things were, but his bike was gone. She hadn't bothered to check her phone, and her body hurt too much to try now. If he had called or sent a text, he would have to wait the way he had made her wait all day.

"I'm making some tea." Cordy poked her head in the living room. "And I called your father. He's on his way down."

"I don't want to see anyone." How could she have been so stupid? Twice in one year she had been attacked. Only tonight she had fought her way off some. If Cordy hadn't shown up when she did, who knew what would have happened? She shuddered, thinking about it.

"Sorry, honey. Your family has a right to know. You should expect your brother too. Maybe even the cousins."

"Oh, please not all of them. I can't handle the entire Wilde family clucking around me at the moment. If the cousins come, tell them to go away." That's the last thing she needed. Sam would want to cite statistics to make himself feel better. Lacey had her own set of problems and didn't need to babysit her. Annabelle was caught up in the bakery at the orchard, and Mac had broken a leg or a knee or something trying to save her cat from the tree. She wanted to be left alone.

Her father burst through the front door. His flannel shirt was undone, revealing his white t-shirt. He had managed to put on jeans, but apparently not any shoes. A crazed look crossed his face. And his hair stood on end.

"Are you okay?" he said. "What do you need me to do? I can have the place watched all night. I'll hire a bodyguard if you want. Cordy, bring me the shotgun."

"Come in the kitchen, Silas. She wants to rest." Cordy ushered him out of the room. She was grateful for her grandmother and her ability to remain calm in a crisis.

She closed her eyes and willed sleep to come. The police had taken a statement. She hadn't had enough of a description for them. Her attacker could have been anyone. Anyone who hated Caleb. The cameras on the building weren't working. The likelihood the police would find out who the man in the ski cap was, was little. At least she had clocked him with the knitting needles. Those stupid things had come in handy for once.

The front door eased open. He was there in his leather jacket with his helmet tucked under his arm. Circles surrounded his hooded eyes. He looked as worn out as she felt, but she was never so happy to see him.

"Where have you been?" Her voice croaked against her throat. She could use that tea after all.

"Are you sick?" He came to her.

"Something like that." She forced herself to sit up and winced.

He dropped down beside her on the sofa. "Were you hurt? What happened?"

"Where were you all day?" She didn't want to talk about what had happened until he answered her question. She needed him, and he had abandoned her.

"I...I...went for a ride."

"That's it? That's all you've got for me?" She pushed up off the sofa and hobbled out to the front porch. She didn't want to have the conversation with her dad and Cordy only feet away. Cordy would listen.

"I did go for a ride. I drove all the way to Cape May and back."

No wonder he looked like week-old fruit. He would have driven close to five hours to do that trip, and he was still pretty banged up from the night someone jumped him. But she didn't understand why he would even think to make a trip like that. "Why didn't you call me or text me back? I tried you several times. You acted like such a jerk earlier today too. What's going on with you?"

She had believed their feelings for each other were real. She had given herself to him because she had trusted him, and today he disappeared like fog on the lake. She had even tried him again when the police had arrived at the craft store. She had needed to hear his voice to give her the strength to face what happened.

"I got spooked. I'm sorry. I asked Jameson for a job today. He told me no one in town would hire me. I went to the orchard to talk with your uncle. I know it's him that's behind this campaign to keep me out of Candlewood Falls."

"How do you know? I mean, how do you really know? I spoke with Brad. He told me what you did today at the orchard, and how Huck reacted. Brad doesn't think he's involved."

Caleb opened his mouth, but she put a hand up. "I'm not

saying my uncle is any kind of angel, because we all know he isn't. But he's not a liar, Caleb. He has no reason to lie. He would admit without regret what he did. He hasn't exactly made it a secret he wants you out of town."

"Then who? Who would do this to me? Sabotage any chance I have of making a life with you. Isn't that what you want?"

"I did. Until earlier today on the street, then you ignored me all day. I needed you tonight. I needed you to be the person who was there for me. And you weren't."

"I'm sorry. What happened? Did you get in a car accident?"

She didn't have the energy to spill the details. Someone else could tell him. "It doesn't matter. You weren't there. And the worst part of it all is you ran when you got scared. How do I know you won't always run? Or run when things get hard? I can't build a life with someone I can't trust to be by my side." Her heart shattered as the words fell from her mouth. She wanted to build a life with him, but how could they manage that? He wasn't ready, and maybe she wasn't either.

Her body shook as the shock wore off. Her head hurt, and her chest hurt. She wanted nothing more than to throw herself into his strong and capable arms, but how could she trust him now? He had left her because he couldn't handle the pressure. If he knew what had happened tonight, he'd be gone again before morning.

"Please don't say we're through. Let me make it up to you. I'll do anything. I won't run anymore. I promise. I realized when I got to the edge of the boardwalk and there was nowhere else to go, the only place I really wanted to be was with you. You have given me a home."

"No, I gave you a place to stay until your bike was fixed. I need to lie down. I'm not feeling well." She fought the tears that threatened to come. She didn't want to break down in front of him because she would cave and accept his apology. She couldn't.

The only thing she wanted from him was his trust. Trust to keep her safe. If he couldn't do that, what good was he?

Caleb waited until Brooklyn was inside and had closed the door. He didn't know what to do to convince her how he felt about her and how sorry he was for running. He ran a hand through his hair. This whole day had spiraled out of control like his motorcycle crashing in the rain.

Exhaustion weighed his body down. He didn't think he could drive one more mile tonight. He didn't dare knock on the door and ask to sleep in his old bed. She had made her position regarding him clear. In the morning, he would pack up the rest of his stuff and leave. Everyone in town would have what they wanted. He'd be gone, and they could go back to believing the worst in him.

He wanted to know what had happened to her tonight. He gave her car and Cordy's car a quick once-over. Neither one had any damage to it. Had she been in an accident in another car? Had she fallen? A cold chill ran down his spine. Had someone hurt her?

Headlights bounced down the driveway. A pickup came to a halt, and Brad jumped out of the truck. Great. Exactly what he needed now.

"Is she all right?" Brad ran around the front of the truck and up the porch steps. His hair was disheveled as if he were lying on it. His shirt was half tucked in and his scuffed-up work boots were untied.

"I don't know. She won't tell me what happened. Was there an accident?"

Brad narrowed his eyes. "She didn't tell you? What did she say?"

"We had a fight. She's pretty fired up about that. She wouldn't answer my questions." He hated admitting to Brad he'd been kicked to the curb. It had only been earlier today he was laying claim to her and trying to scare off Huck on her behalf. Brad would have himself a good laugh about this. Brad had told him to get lost, and he had been right. Caleb wasn't good enough for Brooklyn.

Brad shook his head. "I probably shouldn't tell you. She's going to get mad at me too, but someone mugged her in the parking lot by the craft store tonight."

His vision blurred red while his fists clenched. Someone had made good on the threats. He was only bringing her harm. He needed to go, but if he got his hands on the person who did that to her, they would never see the light of day again. He would fight until he was the only one standing, to protect her.

"Do they know who did it?" he said.

"He got away. The police don't have any leads," Brad said.

"What did this attacker do to her?" He wanted to run inside and wrap her in his arms, tell her she never had to worry again. He would keep her safe, but he hadn't. He had failed at the one thing he promised her.

Her anger made more sense now. She had been attacked again, and he wasn't there for her because he was running scared. Like a coward. Not like a man. No wonder she felt like she couldn't trust him.

"He hit her a few times. But my sister stabbed the guy with her knitting needles. He was stunned by what she'd done. At that point Cordy had come out, and he took off. She didn't get a good look at him."

Pride for what she'd done filled his chest like helium. His sweet, innocent Brooklyn had taken charge and saved herself.

Had she realized that yet? She didn't really need him at all. But he wanted her to still want him.

"I need to ask a favor." He swallowed the bad taste in his mouth. He never thought he'd be asking Brad Wilde for a favor.

"I don't know if I can help you. I know my sister likes you. She told me so today, but it's your fault this happened to her."

"I know. I'll leave in the morning, but I want to sleep in the gift shop tonight. I'll grab a blanket from the barn and camp out on the floor, if that's okay. I want to be near if she needs anything. Could you get word to Cordy for me, so she doesn't worry if she sees me moving around? I can't go in the house. Brooklyn hates me right now. And I can't drive another mile. I wouldn't ask if I wasn't so bone-tired."

Brad stared at him for a minute. "Can I ask you something first?"

"Sure." He was in no position to negotiate, and every second he stood there, his legs turned to rubber. He wouldn't be able to stand up much longer. Fatigue and worry were having their way with him.

"Did you kill SJ?"

"No." He would have to answer that question for the rest of his life if he stayed in town. Living places where no one knew his history gave him a chance to get out from under the assumption he killed someone and give him a minute of peace. That would be the only good thing about leaving in the morning. He'd go so far no one would have any idea who he was.

"Do you love my sister?"

His feelings for Brooklyn were none of Brad's business. He thought he was falling in love with Brooklyn, but what was the point if she could not love him back? "I want to, but she doesn't feel that way about me."

"You're wrong about that one. Go get some sleep. You look like you're about to fall over. My dad and I are sleeping on the couch tonight. If you hear anything, let me know. I'll do the same." Brad patted him on the shoulder.

They may have passed from total hatred to civility. Or his tired brain had played a trick on him. "Thanks, man," he said and wandered off to the gift shop.

He stopped to check on the alpacas first. Everyone was asleep. He grabbed a blanket and unlocked the store with the key he still had. He would probably regret sleeping on the floor in the morning, but at least he would have one more night with Brooklyn nearby. This time tomorrow he'd be miles away. And lost again.

CHAPTER NINETEEN

Brooklyn threw the blankets off. Sleep hid from her and no amount of looking was going to bring it out of hiding. Thoughts of Caleb and the attack ran in circles in her brain. Her body wished her mind would share some of that energy. Every part of her ached. Especially her heart. She would never see Caleb again. She was going to have to learn to be brave all by herself.

She grabbed her phone and padded down the steps not wanting to wake anyone. Brad had taken the guest room on the first floor where Caleb had slept. Her father had resigned himself to the couch, the shotgun within reach.

She slipped into the kitchen. Dad's snoring drifted down the hall. She guessed Brad would be cutting some wood behind the closed door to the bedroom. Living in that small cabin together when she and Brad were younger had made for some noisy nights. Where was Caleb sleeping tonight? She brought up the last text message to him and let her finger hover above the screen. She was on her own. No calling. No texting. He was a grown man. He could find a place to sleep.

Like her grandmother, she made tea for comfort, but she used the microwave so the tea kettle wouldn't wake her father. She wanted something warm to wrap her hands around more than she wanted to drink it. The cold hadn't left her since the parking lot earlier. She couldn't keep thinking about what happened or what almost happened. She couldn't take any more pain.

She pushed out the screen door onto the back porch. The fall night was damp. The temperatures had dropped even more overnight. No more late summer weather. Thanksgiving would be here before she knew it. And she wouldn't be spending it with Caleb.

An alpaca called out in distress. Her head snapped up, and she strained to hear. Was she imagining the noise? No, Lucy called for help. Brooklyn ran around the front of the house and dropped the tea mug.

The barn. The alpacas. She screamed.

"Fire."

Caleb dragged himself from a deep sleep. His mind fought him at first. He needed to sleep for a few more hours. He had just put his head down on his jacket he used as a pillow. But something was wrong. The nagging feeling, like a child poking him for attention, finally won. He sat up and smelled smoke. Sweat had made his shirt stick to his chest. The temperature in the gift shop must've risen twenty degrees.

He jumped up and threw on his boots. The screeches from the alpacas came right through the floorboards. The barn was on fire. He needed to save the animals.

He barreled down the steps and around to the barn doors. Flames licked and bit the back wall. The heat from the door handle burned his hand. He jumped back.

"Use this." Brad shoved a wet towel in his hand.

"Where is everyone?" He shouted over the roar of the flames.

"Calling the fire department."

He yanked open the barn doors and all five alpacas came running. Alistair knocked into him and sent him tumbling.

Movement caught his eye. "Brad, someone is out there."

"Dad, bring the gun." Brad waved Silas over. Brooklyn ran behind her dad. Cordy stood on the porch.

"Brooklyn, get away from the fire," he said, moving in the direction of what had to be a person running. The silhouette was stocky, but fast. The body shape seemed familiar. Whoever started the fire was getting away. They needed to catch him.

Silas and Brad were fast on his heels. Their labored breaths and pounding footfalls were right behind him and still they couldn't catch the guy.

"Stop," he yelled.

"Catch him, Caleb," Brooklyn said from somewhere behind him. She must have stopped running. He needed to catch this bastard for her. He would put an end to her torment. This arsonist wouldn't harm her anymore.

"I have a gun," Silas said, but that didn't deter the guy.

The man kept running in the direction of the fence. If he jumped it, he would be in the open flat field. He'd be able to pick up speed and get into the tree line. They'd lose him for sure if he made it to the trees.

The man took another step and went airborne, his arms and legs sticking out in all directions. A long stick came up out of the ground and hit him in the face. He fell headfirst into the fence. Caleb skidded to a stop with his heart pounding in his ears. Brad collided into his back with a whoosh. They stumbled but didn't fall.

"What the hell?" Brad said.

Silas pulled up alongside them with the shotgun pointed at the fence.

"He fell." Caleb took a tentative step forward. The other two men flanked him. Whatever tripped this guy had given them a lucky break. He needed his luck to change a little. Now was a good time.

He stole a glance at the barn. The fire still burned. Where was the fire department?

They moved forward another few steps. The man didn't move. He was either trying to deceive them, or he was really out cold.

"Get up nice and slow," Silas said. "I have a shotgun pointed at your head, and I will use it."

The man groaned.

Brad kicked the guy in the leg. "Get up, shithead. You're outnumbered."

The moon cast enough light that he could make out the man better. His hair was short and dark. He wore all black. Everything finally made sense.

"Vetter, show your face," Caleb said.

"What?" Brad said, astounded.

Officer Zahn Vetter pushed up onto his knees and held his head. He groaned again and faced them. Blood ran down his face and dripped off his chin.

"Holy shit, it was Vetter all along," Brad said.

"He's been trying to pin the robbery on me. You thought a fire to Brooklyn's barn would do what? Get me in trouble for arson and robbery?" He allowed the burn inside his veins to take over. He gripped Vetter by the back of the shirt and pulled him off the ground. His fist collided with Vetter's jaw, making the man's head snap back.

Brad pulled him away from Vetter who slumped to the

ground next to the object that had tripped him. Caleb grabbed the rake and laughed.

"What's so funny?" Silas said.

"This is Alistair's rake. He carries it around under his neck and drops it all over the place. It's a game he plays." He choked out another laugh at the irony of Vetter getting stopped by an alpaca. If he didn't love those animals before, he sure as hell loved them all now.

"Use this to tie him up." Weezer River stood on the other side of the fence with a roll of twine in her hand. She was tall and thin, much older than the last time he saw her, and wearing a tan rain coat.

"Weezer, where the hell did you come from?" Silas said.

"I saw the flames from my window. I ran to see what was going on. The twine was in my pocket. Lucky for that. Now tie up this piece of garbage." She shoved the twine at Caleb. He took it and tied Vetter's hands behind his back, then helped him to his knees.

A flash lit up the area like a tiny white explosion. He blinked against the light. Brooklyn stood there pointing her phone at Vetter. "Now we have proof with time and a date. He won't be able to deny his involvement with his police connections."

"Your stupid phone won't mean anything. No one will believe I set that fire." Vetter spit the blood from his mouth.

"But you did," Brooklyn said.

"You're damn right I did. If you and your family won't get rid of this vermin from our town, then I have to. He murdered your uncle and your brother, Silas. He probably robbed Mrs. Holloway too. What kind of a family man are you by allowing this scum to come within a foot of your daughter? If she were my daughter, I would've beat him and her."

Brooklyn hit Vetter across the face with a flat hand. The slap echoed across the field. His heart swelled with pride for how tough she was.

"Who attacked Brooklyn?" He leaned in close to Vetter's face. The smell of iron and sweat poured off him. Caleb would make Vetter tell them who had hurt her, and he wouldn't stop with a closed fist.

"I don't know, and if I did, I wouldn't tell you." Vetter spit on him.

"I'm going to make you tell." He balled his hand and pulled back for a full body punch. His fist stalled. Brooklyn held his hand with force. She shook her head. "No more fighting. He's not worth it."

She was right, but hitting him square on the jaw to make him spill would have felt good. "He tells us, or I do it."

"Oh, for land's sakes." Weezer climbed over the fence, pushing her coat out of the way. She grabbed Vetter by the ear and twisted until he screamed. "Zahn Vetter, you will tell us who attacked Brooklyn, or I swear I'll pull your ear clean off."

"All right. All right. Let go, you crazy buzzard. I sent one of the men from my group, the Brotherhood of Watchmen. Figured getting his woman would do the trick."

Weezer released him. He fell forward on his face with a grunt. Brad helped him to his knees again.

"Does Huck know about this?" Silas continued to hold the gun inches from Vetter's face.

"Huck? Hell, no. That old man doesn't have it in him anymore to get the job done. He's useless. If I had my way, I'd throw him out of the Watchmen and Candlewood Falls on principle."

"You sent the men after me both times." So, it wasn't Huck after all. He almost laughed. Vetter had been acting on his own, directing other members of the Watchmen to come after him. He had believed Huck was the mastermind behind the whole thing, the one telling Vetter what to do.

"What do we do with him?" Brad said.

"We hand him over to the authorities." Brooklyn looked at her brother as if he'd grown a horn out of the middle of his head.

"That's too easy." He wanted Vetter to suffer a little for all that Vetter had put him through, and not just this time, but for last time too. Handing him over to the cops would not provide the right kind of justice, and Vetter was a slippery as oil on gears. He'd walk before any reparations could occur.

"But a cop in prison?" Brad said. "He'd get what was coming to him there."

Silas never let the gun waiver. "We could shoot him. The town doesn't need a bully police officer throwing his weight around. It's the exact thing I've been against for decades."

Vetter winced and ducked his chin.

"Dad!" Brooklyn's eyes widened.

"I'm only joking." Silas winked, but the gun didn't budge. Brad let out a laugh.

The sounds of sirens reverberated in the distance. Time was running out to decide what to do with Vetter if they weren't going to send him to prison.

"I have an idea." He hoped the others would go along with what he was about to propose.

All eyes were on him.

"He should go to jail, but there is a chance he'll get away with setting the fire, and we'll never be able to prove he wants to set me up for the robbery. No one knows better than I do, that justice isn't always served correctly. We don't know his connections and what kind of webs they'll spin to set him free. Then he'll be right back on the streets of Candlewood Falls using his power to do harm. The worst thing to do to Vetter would be to banish him from his treasured town forever."

CHAPTER TWENTY

Brooklyn's hand throbbed. She had hit Vetter across the face with everything she had. He wanted to use violence to make his point? Well, she had had enough of men and their hands hitting and taking what didn't belong to them. Violence wasn't the answer to violence, but hitting him sure made her insides hum. Kind of made her a hypocrite since she had stopped Caleb from doing the same. She didn't want him to get into anymore trouble. And not on her account.

The fire continued to work its way through the barn. The fire truck's sirens grew louder. Help would be there soon. She'd have to rebuild, but at least the alpacas were safe.

"How are we going to keep Vetter out of town never to return?" she said. Nothing could ease her worry more than knowing she would never have to run into Vetter again. She would much rather he leave town than Caleb. Even if she and Caleb couldn't be together, he should stay in Candlewood Falls and make a life for himself. This was his home, and it had been taken from him.

Caleb motioned for them to follow him. Silas remained

with the gun still pointed at Vetter. Weezer joined the group too. She had certainly earned the right after making Vetter talk. They would need to have their story straight, if they let Vetter go. She still wasn't sure it was a good idea.

"Brooklyn, are you with us?" Caleb said.

"What? Yes. Sorry. Go ahead. You were saying."

"We have the photo of Vetter that Brooklyn took putting him on the property at the time of the fire. Brad and I saw him run away from the barn. That makes two eyewitnesses. If he wasn't guilty, he wouldn't have run."

"He could make something up," Brad said.

"He could try, but a prosecutor will believe you and Silas. Your name means credibility in this town. Just as much, if not more than Vetter's. You two saw him running toward the fence. He can't deny that."

"Are you sure we should let him leave and not turn him over to the police? He should pay for what he did to my barn. That's attempted murder, isn't it? He could've killed the alpacas." She shuddered to think about losing her special pets. They were just as much family as Brad or Cordy or her dad...or Caleb.

"A more severe punishment for him would be to have to start over somewhere else. This town and abusing his power in it are the most important things to him," Caleb said.

"But what if he tries to hurt people in another town?" She tried to get her head around what Caleb was suggesting. Her instincts to follow the rules wanted to kick in, but maybe this time, doing things their way was better.

"He won't have the same power in another town," Brad said. "He can't explain why he left the police force. Anywhere new would want references. He's only something in Candlewood Falls. Everywhere else he's nobody."

"He goes now. In the middle of the night with no explanation," Silas said.

"We let him go, but he can't ever come back," Caleb said.

"Are you sure?" she said.

"I think we should shoot him," Weezer said.

"Weezer, we're not shooting him," Brad said.

"What if he won't go? And what about police friends who could get him another job? He could go into private security." There were too many variables. Anything could go wrong with this idea. They couldn't trust Vetter. "What if he comes back for you worse than before?"

"He won't," Silas said. "I moved closer so I could hear you. We do Caleb's idea. I have the ace in the hole."

"What's that, Dad?" Brad said.

"My good for nothing brother just became good for something. He's going to prove his allegiance to his family instead of his group of ignorant men."

They moved back to Vetter who was still kneeling and bleeding. Each one of them stood there, staring him down. The arrogant look on his face had changed to something more like fear.

"Here's the deal," Caleb began. "You're going to leave town tonight. And you're never coming back to Candlewood Falls. If you so much as step a toe over the town line, we'll bring all the evidence we have against you to the county sheriff's office, the fire marshal, and the press."

"I'm going to insist my brother keeps you out of town, and believe me, my brother will listen. He and his men—not yours—will watch for you. And if I get even a whiff that you're throwing your weight around, I'll have them hunt you down. I'll be there with this gun, and I won't be as gracious as I am tonight," Silas said.

"You can't throw me out of my own town. I won't go."

Caleb grabbed Vetter by his hair and pulled. Vetter cried out. "You are going to go because you believe I'm capable of killing someone. If you think I would kill poor SJ Wilde who was nothing more than a hurting man, be good and certain I will not hesitate to end you. You are leaving town. Am I clear enough for you?"

"I've got nowhere to go."

"That's the idea. You tried to run me out of town for weeks since I stopped at the bar and for no good reason. You had a hatred for me my whole life because I look different, I sound different, and I am different. Instead of coming after me, you should've figured out who killed your friend. You have two seconds to take our deal."

The fire truck pulled onto the driveway. Cordy ran from the porch toward the truck, waving her hands. The alpacas stayed huddled by the side of the house.

"I'll be gone by morning."

"You'll be gone in an hour," Caleb said.

"Fine. An hour." Vetter stared at the ground.

"How can we trust him?" She grabbed Caleb's arm. He flinched, and she dropped her hand. It really was over between them. She wasn't sure if she would be able to get over him. She had fallen hard for him, instead of doing a better job to guard her heart.

"Because I'm going to escort him to the county line," Silas said.

"And like Silas said, if we get word he's up to his old ways, I'm reporting him. He doesn't want to go to prison. I can't be the only person he wrongly accused. If he comes back, he loses. And he loses by staying away. You don't have to worry anymore. He won't hurt you again."

Vetter's feelings about Caleb and her weren't much of a surprise. For a brief second, she believed her uncle had orchestrated it all, even her assault at the craft store, but Vetter had rounded up the men to torture them. Vetter was full of hatred and poison like a black widow spider. She might be safe now, but she lost Caleb.

Brad pulled Vetter to his feet. "You better get moving. The police won't be far behind the fire department."

"Untie me." Vetter held up his hands.

"Untie yourself," Weezer said. "You got a lucky deal, Officer Vetter. I wouldn't have been so kind to you if you had set my property on fire."

Brad shoved Vetter who stumbled, but righted himself, his hands still tied together.

"You tell the fire department or the police I followed the man who ran away. We'll say I couldn't catch him. Everyone understand?" Silas handed the gun to Brad.

They all agreed.

"But Dad, are you sure? I don't want you to get in trouble," she said.

"If anyone is going to lie to the authorities, it's me." Dad hugged her and Brad. He stuck a hand out to Caleb. "When I'm wrong, I say it. I'm sorry for mistrusting you. Now, I'm asking you to take care of my daughter."

Caleb shook his hand. "You have my word, sir."

With a nod, Silas followed Vetter until they hit the tree line and disappeared.

"What are we going to tell the fire department?" she said. She hadn't thought about that until now. They had begun spraying water on the barn. Men in turnout gear ran from the trucks to the barn. "We're all out here in the field. That's going to raise some questions."

"He could've used an accelerant," Brad said. "That's going to make someone poke around."

"We say we didn't see who did it, but a man ran this way and into the tree line. Silas went after him. When Silas returns, he'll say he lost whoever it was. There will be a hunt for the person who started the fire. If Vetter's lucky, he gets out of town in time. If he isn't, they figure out he did it," Caleb said.

"I still don't understand why you wanted to let him go." She was certain he would want justice on the man who had hurt him, if not for her than at least for himself.

"Believe me, us getting the better of him, of me being able to stay in his town when he has to leave is the best punishment possible. And we can always give an anonymous tip to the police or the fire marshal. He'll get his either way." Caleb grabbed the rake. "We have good old Alistair to thank for the extra help. I'm going to give that fuzzy animal a big kiss."

CHAPTER TWENTY-ONE

The sun split the sky into rows of pinks and oranges. The fire department had left. The barn was a ruined mess of burnt wood and puddles filled with dirt and hay. At least her precious alpacas were safe. Brad had loaded them up in the trailers and brought them to the orchard for now. She had given Alistair a big hug for helping to save the day. He hummed in return.

Brooklyn sat on the front steps of the house. Her body was one gigantic ache from the last twelve hours or so. She couldn't believe they had caught Vetter and let him go. Hopefully, they don't live to regret that decision.

She didn't understand why someone could be so filled with hate for another person for no good reason. The idea was pointless, and yet she had seen it time and again. The world made little sense most days. At least the farm gave her a purpose. She would cling to that in the days ahead as she began to rebuild the barn and parts of her life.

"Cordy thought you might like this." Caleb handed her a mug of herbal tea. Cordy had thought of her and what she might need, not him. He had given up on her so quickly. She willed her face to hide the disappointment and wrapped her hands around the mug for its warmth. She inhaled the crisp smell of orange and cranberry tea. He sat beside her on the step with a mug of his own.

"I'm glad you stayed in the gift shop last night. If you hadn't been there, something might've happened to the animals." The relief when she had seen him directing the alpacas away from the fire had almost brought her to her knees.

"Lucky, I guess. Things are pretty much in control here now. I won't hang around. I know you want your space. I just wanted to make sure you're okay."

"I will be." She would be better if he was with her, but that wasn't possible. She had said some terrible things to him and couldn't unsay them. She had believed he wasn't there for her after the yarn store incident. He had proved her very wrong after that.

"If you ever need anything, call me. I'll always help you." He stood, leaving a soft kiss on the top of her head. "I'm sorry."

She was the one who had something to be sorry for. She stood too. "Where are you going? Aren't you staying in town?" After all that he had fought for, how could he leave now?

He shoved his hands in his pockets. "I don't think I will. With Vetter and me gone, no one will bother you. And you have your dad and brother to watch out for you."

"Is that all I was for you, some charity case?"

"I know I screwed up by leaving without saying anything. For a second I lost it or went a little crazy. No one has ever meant to me what you do. For years, I've kept myself away from people not to get attached, but one second in your company, and I was hooked. I thought if I left, I would save you some pain. But I realized that I was

215

being an ass. I'm sorry I wasn't here when you called. I should've been."

"I'm sorry too for the things I said. I was mad last night because I was hurt and scared. I had been scared all day, actually. You acted so weird outside the coffee shop, and I couldn't figure out why at first. I was coming home to talk to you about it when I got attacked. That wasn't on you. I didn't mean to send you away."

"I was acting like a coward, but when I stood on that boardwalk, I knew the only place I wanted to be was with you. You're my home, Brooklyn. If I can't come home to you, then I can't stay in Candlewood Falls. This place will never be home without you."

He said all the right things. Her heart believed him and longed to go to him, but her mind gave one last protest. Trusting could mean getting hurt. She had had enough pain to last her a lifetime. But not being with Caleb opened a chasm in her chest that might never close. She had never expected to fall in love with him again. She hadn't even expected to see him again, but fate or something had brought them together. If there was any silver lining in what had happened to her last year, it was finding Caleb.

She closed the space between them and tilted up her chin. "I realized something too."

"What's that?" He smirked and raised a brow.

"I can be brave all by myself. I love the idea that you want to protect me, and I'd like for you to do that once in a while, but last night, twice, I took care of myself and did okay with it. I shook in my shoes, but I fought back. I stabbed that guy with my needles, and I stood up to Vetter."

"You smacked him pretty good." Caleb laughed and ran a finger down her arm. Her skin tingled with his touch, a touch she wanted every day.

"You don't have to be my knight in shining armor. But I

would like it if you would stay here with me and build a life together." She held her breath, but let it go, trusting and believing.

"I'll never be mister popular around here. Someone will always wonder why you're with me when you could be with anyone. Someone better."

"There is no one better for me. I don't care what anyone thinks. I want you, the man with a heart as big as this county, the man who stands up for what's right even when it's hard, the man who has my back, who accepts me as I am." That last part was the most important. He knew about what happened in her past, and he didn't judge her. He had done the opposite. He had shown her love and respect, made her feel like a whole woman again.

He cupped her face and kissed her. "I would like nothing more than to come home to you night after night."

"Can I convince you to sleep in my bed tonight?" She wrapped her arms around his neck and pressed against him.

"With your grandmother in the house? No way." He choked out a laugh.

"Then there's only one respectable thing we can do." She hadn't thought of this before, but what the heck. She never wanted to allow fear to stop her again. This time she would jump into life with both feet, laughing the whole way down. With Caleb.

"What are you saying?" He narrowed his eyes.

"Marry me." She had never said anything so spontaneous in her life. Like her grandmother, her intuition moved her to act, to live in the moment without regret. She wasn't like her mother, not in the way she had believed. She had a lot more of Cordy in her.

"Aren't we rushing things a little?" He brushed the hair away from her face.

"I don't think so. This feels right." *Oh, yes it did.* Righter than anything had felt in a long time.

"Don't you want me to ask the question?"

"Why? Because you're the guy?"

"I thought you might want me to get down on one knee, or ask your dad first, or something like that." He pulled her close.

She kissed him, relishing his mouth and the soft moan he made when the kiss went deeper. "I don't care about a traditional proposal, but if you want to give me that, I won't stop you. I just want to be with you, right there inside that house. You, me, and the alpacas." Maybe a bigger family in the future, but one step at a time, of which they had plenty.

"My answer then, Brooklyn Wilde, is yes. Let's go home."

READY FOR ANOTHER TRIP TO CANDLEWOOD FALLS?

If you would like to see more of Weezer River's antics and how she tries to save her winery please check out Rivers Edge by USA Today best selling author Jen Talty.

And if you want to spend some time with Brooklyn's cousin Sam Wilde and his quest for an apple to make you happy and horny, you'll want to read Wilde Temptation by K.M. Fawcett.

Spend the holidays with Lacey Wilde, her dog Remi, and a sexy marine who claims Remi belongs to him in WILDE CHRISTMAS by K.M. Fawcett.

What will Brad Wilde—the man who has it all—do when an orphan is dropped on his doorstep? Raising Winter by Stacey Wilk.

Some truths weren't meant to be uncovered. THE BURIED SECRET by Jen Talty

Thank you for visiting Candlewood Falls!

Be sure to leave a review to help readers like you find and enjoy our small town.

Join our exciting community of authors and readers at the Candlewood Falls Facebook Readers Group for cover reveals, sneak peaks, deleted scenes, and excerpts from upcoming releases. Plus games and fun!

ACKNOWLEDGMENTS

No book is ever written alone. Even though for Taking Root, I did the research about alpacas by myself, I still had a little help with making the story even better. First I have to thank K.M. Fawcett and Jen Talty for partnering with me on this project and for all the brainstorming we did to make my plot as solid as it could be. I would also like to thank my incomparable Beta Reader—Robin Rottner for her amazing feedback. Always. And my talented editor Kimberly Dawn. And of course, I have to thank my constant readers. For without you, there is no one to hear my stories. Thank you from the bottom of my heart for sharing your free time with me.

∾

ABOUT THE AUTHOR

From an early age, Stacey Wilk told tales as a way to escape. At six she wrote short stories in composition notebooks, at twelve she wrote a novel on a typewriter, in high school biology she wrote rock star romances in her binder instead of paying attention.

But it wasn't until many years later, inspired by her children and a looming birthday, that she finally took her story-telling seriously. And published her first novel in 2013. Since then, she's gone on to publish seventeen more so women everywhere could fall in love and find an escape of their own.

She isn't done telling stories. Not by a long shot. If you want to read her emotional and honest books about family, romance, and second chances, visit her at www.staceywilk.com

~

ALSO BY STACEY WILK

The Heritage River Series

A Second Chance House

The Bridge Home

The Essence of Whiskey and Tea

The Brotherhood Protectors World

Winter's Last Chance

The Last Betrayal

Her Last Word

The Last Days of Christmas

Seduced by Denial

Winter at the Shore

No More Darkness

Through the Darkness

Light Upon the Darkness

Darkness Until Dawn (Coming 2022)

The Big Sky Country Series

Time Won't Erase

Stay Awhile (Coming Soon)

Book #3 (2022)

Book #4 (2022)

Made in the USA
Columbia, SC
26 September 2022